He tilted her chin up toward his face.

"You are a remarkable woman," he whispered and kissed her forehead lightly.

As they walked slowly through the torch-lit streets, Marco yearned to hold her closely in his arms. But he knew it was not yet time. Perhaps there would never be a time. They had only tonight for certain. The warmth of the afternoon sun had faded, and a chilling wind began to whip their cloaks. All too soon the dolphin fountain came into view. They arrived at the side entrance, where Sylvia was waiting to open the door for Bianca.

Marco put his hands on Bianca's shoulders and looked down into her upturned face. "I will never forget this evening. Thank you, Bianca, for staying. I will see you again?"

"Yes, Marco."

His hands slid down her arms and clasped her hands. They stood for several moments, searching each other's face. Fire from the street torch reflected in their eyes, burning forever a glow into their memories that would last a lifetime. Slowly Marco let his hands drop from hers, whispered "good night," and disappeared into the darkness.

W9-DEW-321

BARBARA YOUREE has authored three children's books as well as numerous stories and articles. She is Contributing Editor of *Potpourri, A Magazine of the Literary Arts* and a docent at the Nelson-Atkins Museum of Art. *Both Sides of the Easel* is her first inspirational novel. She makes her home in Kansas.

Both Sides of the Easel

Barbara Youree

Heartsong Presents

Grateful thanks to Marilyn Collins, Dale Hausmann, Richard Kennison, Geri Norton, and Esther Tuttle, who took time and care to review this manuscript. And warm appreciation to family and friends for their continued encouragement.

A note from the author:
I love to hear from my readers! You may correspond with me by writing: **Barbara Youree**
Author Relations
PO Box 719
Uhrichsville, OH 44683

ISBN 1-58660-155-5

BOTH SIDES OF THE EASEL

Scripture taken from the HOLY BIBLE: NEW INTERNATIONAL VERSION®. NIV®. Copyright© 1973, 1978, 1984 by International Bible Society. Used by permission of Zondervan Publishing House.

With the exception of renouned historical figures, all of the characters and events in this book are fictitious. Any resemblance to actual persons, living or dead, or to actual events is purely coincidental.

Cover illustration by Randy Hamblin

PRINTED IN THE U.S.A.

one

Rome, early 1600s

"Bianca Maria, dear daughter, come inside," Stefano Marinelli called from the garden doorway. "I have some most interesting news."

So absorbed was the young woman in her sketch of a scarlet rose, it took a few moments for the words to register. By that time her father had strolled across the courtyard and had settled beside her on the stone bench. Bianca had become most precious to him since the recent loss of his eldest son. She had been the only one who could console his pain—bring a smile back to his life. He doted on her, indulged her beyond all reason.

"You are as lovely as a painting yourself," he said, noting her classic pose, her dark ringlets blithely tumbling about her shoulders as she leaned over her wax tablet.

"Oh, Papa," she scolded. "You know I would rather *do* a painting than *be* one. Her playful eyes looked up at him; they were set in the exquisite face of the woman she was too rapidly becoming. "So what's on that bit of parchment in your hand? I hope it is not from a suitor who thinks of me as his perfect spouse."

"No, no, my dear daughter. Though at sixteen, you know we must again be thinking of a suitable betrothal. It grieves me greatly that Roland was swept away by the plague in Milan. He was so right for you."

"I don't grieve, Papa. We hardly knew each other. What's on that little card?"

"I'm going to make you guess," he said, his eyes twinkling

as he tucked the square of parchment behind him. "Who is the most controversial, the most admired—but most often rejected—and probably the *best* young artist in Rome today?"

"Michele Merisi da Caravaggio, of course! You know I esteem him above all others!" Bianca had followed Caravaggio's rapid rise to fame, studying each new painting as it appeared for public viewing. His holy pictures were denounced by some as too real, too much like the people they knew. Others praised his naturalism as bringing the Scriptures to the understanding of all. In fantasy Bianca had created the complete and ideal man that surely this fabulous artist must be.

"Then perhaps you would like to meet him?"

"Oh, Papa, don't tease me so."

"Your mother and I have been invited by the Contarelli family—an invitation that does, of course, include any child of ours—to a special service to dedicate the three new paintings in their private chapel in the Church of San Luigi dei Francesci."

"The huge St. Matthew paintings? And the great Caravaggio himself will be there?"

"Yes, and yes," Signor Marinelli replied, delighting in his daughter's enthusiasm but totally unaware of her accompanying fantasy.

"When? What shall I wear? Suddenly my little rose sketch seems so puny. . . ," she sputtered.

"It is to take place late Sunday afternoon. I have no idea what you will wear, but I'm sure you will be beautiful. And, no, you are mistaken; this little rose. . ." He took the wax tablet and studied it closely. "You have made it so real. It reaches up to you right out of the wax, as if begging to be plucked. No, your sketch is not puny."

"Thank you, Papa," she said, quietly savoring his all-too-rare compliment on her artistic efforts.

Stefano returned the tablet and, quickly changing his tone, reminded his daughter, "I believe your mother is ready for you to help in the cheese making."

❧

"Sautez, dansez, embrassez qui vous voudrez," Bianca's mother, Françoise, sang as she rhythmically stepped around the table that held the cheese tub.

"Mother, you are, indeed, in high spirits this morning," Bianca said, laughing as she entered the large kitchen and picked up a wooden paddle.

Embarrassed by being caught at private merrymaking, the dignified Françoise blushed and patted the curd firmly against the side of the wooden tub. "It's the smell of the goat cheese, I suppose," she said as though explaining the cause and effect of fire or flood. "It brings back the gay times when I was a girl in France. It was my job to milk the goats." A long pause. "My mother, aunts, and female cousins—we would all make goat cheese together, like this."

"And sing that French ditty about dancing and kissing whomever you would wish?" Bianca teased, squeezing the whey from the curd with her wooden paddle. Her mother rarely spoke of her childhood, and Bianca hoped to squeeze a little more of it from her.

"I do hope we have enough molds for all this cheese," Françoise said to the four walls, ignoring Bianca's stark translation of the folk song.

For her part, Bianca realized she had come too close to her mother's sensitivities. She knew why her mother made her own French cheese—no one in all of Italy could equal it. Neither spoke as they labored on either side of the tub. But the tune continued to whirl around in Bianca's head to the rhythm of the patting: *Kiss whom-ev-er you would wish.* She had just told her father she didn't grieve over Roland's death, which was true, but she did often wonder if she could have grown to love him as her husband. He was a good man. The few times they had met, he had seemed somewhat distant and formal, but never rude or unkind.

What she did remember vividly was the one kiss that night in the moonlight, in the courtyard. His lips were eager, soft, and warm as they pressed against hers. The feelings that had exploded within her were not, she was certain, from love for Roland. But the kiss had left a longing, a passion, that found no place to settle. So she lumped it in with the one desire she could understand—art.

❧

Far away from this domestic scene, four men sat in a Madrid tavern, plotting.

"Another round of *cerveza, señorita!*" called out Jacopo, the apparent leader of the group.

An agile, young woman quickly produced four tankards of beer and set them in the middle of the table.

"Here ye go, wench," one of the men said with a leer, dropping gold coins down the front of her blouse and winking at his comrades.

Blushing, she swirled to leave, but not in time to escape a swat on her backside.

"Don't be hasty," Jacopo called after her. They all laughed uproariously.

"Another drink to our success!" said one, as they all raised their tankards.

"To King Philip!" Clink.

"Who is too ignorant to know his gold finds a home in our pouches!" Clink.

"And too weak to supervise his underlings!" Clink.

They drank heartily, all the while howling at their own perverted jokes.

"Since ridding the world of Roberto was such a smooth and profitable endeavor, what have we learned for this next commission?" said Jacopo, suddenly sobering. The gaunt man with a pointed black beard looked older than his thirty-seven years.

"Me, I've learnt we 'ad to wait too long for the award,"

said one. That brought more guffaws and made it doubly hard for Jacopo to regain their attention.

"We were all amply paid," said Jacopo. "Roberto will no longer be prying into what is not his business. We have, in fact, defended the Empire from heretical ideas."

"Down with heresy!" the three others shouted in unison, raising their empty tankards.

Finally Jacopo was able to get their attention—or at least their glassy stares. He retraced how they had carried out the murder of Roberto, how they had made necessary adjustments to the ambush plan to compensate for weaknesses.

In time Jacopo planned to become the sole proprietor of a vast seigniory in Italy, owning lush vineyards and a lifetime of fortune. But until this could be accomplished, he found it thrilling to support his lavish lifestyle in Spain by such hazardous pursuits in the underworld.

two

Bianca stepped out on the little balcony that overlooked the villa's courtyard. Sunlight fell softly on her fine-featured face and delightful aromas wafted up from the late blooming plants in Grecian urns below. She breathed in the crisp autumn air and felt invigorated. The red-tile roofs of Rome were etched against an intense blue sky, and in the far distance, across the Tiber, she could see the dome of St. Peter's Basilica. The clatter of carriage wheels over the cobbled streets mixed with the distant shouts of merchants hawking their wares. It was a wonderful time to live in Rome.

The past few years Bianca had yearned to be more than a witness from this balcony to the great explosion of painting and architecture. She felt an urgency to learn and develop her God-endowed talents. But, alas, she struggled against dual barriers: being a woman and lacking a master teacher.

But this afternoon, as church bells throughout the city signaled the end of siesta, the thrill of anticipation engulfed her. Rome again stood on the brink of becoming the greatest city in the world. And *she* stood at the precipice of meeting in person the greatest of painters. This just might be the opening of the door that would allow her to become apprenticed to Caravaggio—the ultimate joy, the fulfillment of all her deep longings.

There *were* a few women artists—perhaps, just perhaps, she could become one too. Tutored by both her parents—in Italian and in French—she had already achieved literacy far beyond that of most girls. Because she had been shielded from the outside world most of her childhood, reading had opened a world of dreams for her and lured her toward far-reaching ambitions.

Drawing in a deep breath in an attempt to savor the moment, Bianca took a sweeping glance over her city and slipped back through the French doors into her bedroom.

A tap on the inner door let her know it was time.

"Come in, Sylvia," Bianca called. For as long as she could remember, the servant woman and her now fourteen-year-old son, Albret, had been with the family. An event like the one taking place this afternoon would require her special touches in preparation.

"I'll sit here by the open doors, Sylvia. You can see better to braid my hair."

"*Si, signorina*, I know you never tire of gazing over *your* city." The woman laughed. "I hear you're finally going to meet the big artist man." Sylvia began combing out the long, curling locks.

"Sylvia, what would I do without you to confide in? Don't say a word to Papa, but more than anything I would love to learn to paint in Caravaggio's workshop."

"*Signorina*, he never denies you anything. Why don't you just ask him?

"But, what if he did say no? I know he loves me deeply, but he does have strong beliefs about a woman's place." Following a long, thoughtful pause, Bianca continued. "I've been waiting for the most opportune time. I need to know more about Caravaggio, about his workshop, and I must catch Papa at just the right moment."

"Perhaps that will be this afternoon," encouraged Sylvia.

"Perhaps."

❧

The braids were finally circled around the back of Bianca's head, giving her a more mature look. With Sylvia's help she pulled on an emerald green dress. The snug bodice modestly enhanced her femininity, the collar open in front and turned up in back. The sleeves puffed out at the shoulders, then tapered down firmly to her wrists. The full skirt opened the complete length in front to reveal a pale beige, silk under-dress that Bianca had embroidered herself.

"Sylvia, do you think Caravaggio might notice me?" Bianca asked in an anxious tone, all the while admiring her petite figure in the oval glass.

"And why wouldn't any young gentleman of means notice you, *signorina*," Sylvia said, laughing at the obvious. Bianca smiled into the mirror and imagined the handsome artist standing behind her, his hand resting softly on her shoulder.

Sylvia escorted her down the stairs to the sitting room, where her parents were in low-voiced conversation.

"Bianca Maria, how perfectly gorgeous, how stunning you are, my princess," gushed Signor Marinelli.

Her mother agreed. "You will indeed be a beautiful bride one day, Bianca."

"But, Mother, you know that since Roland's death I've not been able to think of another. . . ." She caught herself slanting the truth.

"Maybe not, but you are nevertheless in love—with parchment and charcoal, and even your little reusable wax tablet. Bianca, your father and I have just been discussing your future. Marriage is the only suitable path for a woman. My father indulged me as does your father. He taught me to play the harpsichord and lute, and all it brought me was sorrow, devastation, and shattered dreams."

"My sweet Françoise, you can still play—and do so from time to time," broke in Stefano. "It's when you came up with the bizarre idea of entering the masculine realm of compos-ing, that. . ."

"Yes, and that is precisely why I want to spare our only daughter the same anguish."

"As do I. Shall we be on our way?" Stefano said, rising and thus terminating the discussion.

Bianca could feel her cheeks flush. *This discussion is not terminated in my mind*, she thought. *I will find a time; I must—it is my life.* It was not anger toward her parents that was burning inside her breast—she loved them both dearly—but rather their acceptance without question of the way things were. She had heard her mother's story dozens of times, but today it seemed to have special significance.

Because the church was not far and the weather was agreeable, her parents had decided to walk from their villa on Via Margutta rather than take their carriage. Bianca strode beside them in silence. Her mother at one time must have felt exactly the same as Bianca did now; she, too, had been a young woman of talent who faced seemingly insurmountable odds. Had *she* just given in without a fight? Or was it her mysterious girlhood in France that colored her story? Her mother completely avoided that subject. Was she equally bitter over her powerlessness? Bianca looked over at her parents as if seeing them for the first time. What a handsome couple they made. Her father wore his black velvet hat with fine feather, brocaded doublet, and well-fitting hosen; his black cape was thrown jauntily over his shoulders. His short, pointed beard was just beginning to gray. Had he always wanted to be a banker with the Medicis, or did he, too, have other dreams? Her mother stood tall and elegant in her dark rose dress, the sleeves trimmed with spiral puffings and a ruff about the neck in the French manner. What secrets did her mother guard behind those tight lips?

They were now approaching San Luigi dei Francesi, the national church of the French who were exiled in Rome. "Bianca Maria, do you know anything about the three paintings of St. Matthew we are about to enjoy?" Stefano asked, breaking the silence.

"Only the news Albret brings me from the streets. While I am sketching in the piazza, he is running around, chatting with anyone whose sleeve he can snatch. He says the altarpiece of 'St. Matthew and the Angel' was rejected because the saint looked like an untutored man of the streets with his big, bare feet. But Caravaggio replaced it with a more elegant version." Bianca's excitement over meeting the great artist had returned, and she was happy to converse pleasantly, without resentment.

"From the few paintings we have seen of his, it amazes me how he can take humble-looking folk and imbue them with such dignity—no halos, no attributes. . . ," commented Stefano.

"Albret says he can only paint when he has a live model in front of him."

"That must be quite an honor to the people he chooses to pose for him," mused Françoise, not wishing to be excluded from the conversation.

"No doubt," Stefano and Bianca chimed together.

Inside the narthex, a mixture of perhaps thirty subdued voices in French and Italian—sprinkled with a bit of Latin—filled the air as greetings were exchanged. Indeed, this was the Marinelli parish church, and the family knew a large number of the invited guests.

"*Madame Cointrel, enchantée de vous voir,*" Bianca heard her mother say to their hostess, using the French form of Contarelli. "You of course remember our youngest, Bianca. . . ." And so on it went with introductions and pleasantries, but there was no sign of the artist.

Bianca was breathless with anticipation of his arrival and gripped with anxiety that he might not come. She patted her brow with a dainty handkerchief, then tucked it back in the cuff of her sleeve.

Suddenly a large, robust, bearded man burst through the doors. He was well dressed, but in an odd fashion, wearing boots that came to the knee and a floppy dark crimson hat that he doffed with a slight swoop and bow, revealing black locks that tumbled to his shoulders.

Voices hushed as all eyes turned toward the newly arrived. "I am Ranuccio Tomassoni," the man began in an authoritative tone. "I have been sent here by Michele Merisi da Caravaggio to inform you that he has been detained. . .humph. . .he can not be with us this afternoon. You see, we were lunching together. . .and to shorten a tedious story. . .our friend became agitated with the waiter and threw a hot plate of artichokes right in his face. And, therefore, he has been detained." A ripple of laughter spread among those who knew Caravaggio better than the rest.

Bianca's heart seemed to lurch to her throat, leaving a hollow void in her chest. Her cherished dreams crumpled like parchment, discarded when one of her drawings had failed.

"And therefore," Tomassoni continued, "is Master Orazio Gentileschi among us?"

"Yes, yes, I am here." The well-respected artist waved his hand from the back of the narthex.

"Caravaggio has requested, Master Gentileschi, if it pleases you, that since you are well schooled in the manner of painting he is attempting to launch, you honor the assembly, following the service, of course, with a few enlightening words about the St. Matthew paintings that are about to be unveiled. I understand from the artist himself that they are his best work to date. Will you so enlighten us, Orazio?" Orazio was a much revered painter in his own right, and, as all knew, his work was highly influenced by the style of Caravaggio.

"Indeed, I shall be honored to do so," Orazio said humbly with a slight bow of the head.

With that, all silently filed into the Contarelli chapel, where the three life-size St. Matthews loomed above and on either side of the altar, reflecting the glory of God. In the hushed interior, as all turned to the unveiled tableaux, a corporate drawing-in of breath sounded like the restrained rushing of wind. Not a word was uttered until after the final amen of the liturgy.

Bianca moved her lips to the words and knelt on cue, but her eyes were riveted to "The Calling of St. Matthew." What a brilliant rendering of the passage! Typical of Caravaggio, the background was quite dark except for a shaft of light that followed Jesus into a room where Matthew, the tax-collector, had been counting coins, surrounded by an odd assortment of characters.

The hand of Jesus as He pointed to His selected disciple, Bianca noticed, was like Michelangelo's hand of God on the Sistine Chapel ceiling, pointing to Adam at creation. Her observations were correct, she learned later, as Orazio was explaining how Caravaggio intended to illustrate that Jesus was indeed creating a spiritual life for Matthew—just as God had created a physical life for Adam.

After the dedication the group of excited admirers, and a few critics eager to express their opinions, filed across the Corso del Rinascimento and down a short distance to the Contarelli villa, where they had all been invited for refreshments. The few children and young adults who had attended gathered in the courtyard. Bianca was seated on some steps next to Orazio's daughter, whom she had just met. Artemisia, though a few years younger than Bianca, knew volumes more than Bianca about art—and about Caravaggio.

"Oh, yes, I have met him. In fact, he has come several times to my father's studio," Artemisia said with a hint of boastfulness in her voice.

"Does Caravaggio show your father how he is able to make parts of the painting appear to come right out of the picture and reach out toward you?" Bianca wanted to know.

"Well, he has made suggestions, but mostly my father just goes to churches and studies his work. As I do."

"Do you like to draw, Artemisia?"

"You know, Bianca, that there are many Caravaggisti—artists who are following his manner of painting—but I intend to be the one *Caravaggista*."

"I thought I was the only girl in all of Rome with such an ambition!" exclaimed Bianca, feeling for the first time in her sheltered life that she had found a kindred spirit.

"Then, certainly there will be room for two Caravaggistas,"

her new-found friend said with graceful generosity. "My father has helped me all along with my drawings, but now he is teaching me how to grind and mix the oil paints. Soon he will show me how to use the paints and all else he knows."

"How very lucky you are, Artemisia!" exclaimed Bianca. "My father, dear as he is, thinks of my art interest as a passing fancy. I'm quite sure he would never let me be apprenticed to anyone. Do you know if it is very difficult to gain an apprenticeship with Caravaggio?"

"You *are* ambitious, my friend!" Artemisia laughed in admiration. "No, I do not know anything about Caravaggio's workshop. Except that he has a cellar for a studio in some palace where he lives under the patronage of Cardinal del Monte. And I know he is a very handsome and charming man."

At that moment the girls were forced to bid each other good-bye as Bianca's father approached with a friendly-looking gentleman.

"Carlo, this is my daughter, Bianca Maria. Bianca, please make the acquaintance of Carlo Maderno. He is creating a new style of architecture with the façade of the church of Santa Suzanna. Because of your interest in art, he has invited both of us to drop by tomorrow afternoon, and he will show us his work."

"I am delighted to meet you, *signore*, and thank you. I shall be most happy to see your new creation," Bianca said with a polite smile.

෨

As the family strolled back to Via Margutta, Bianca tried to sort out the mix of emotions she'd experienced during the evening. The paintings had left an awesome impact. Meeting Artemisia had been a most pleasant and encouraging experience. But what kind of man throws artichokes at a waiter? Surely the great Caravaggio had been greatly provoked, as only the great can be. The devastation of not meeting him lay heavily on her heart.

three

Yesterday, Bianca spared not the slightest detail in her preparation to meet Caravaggio, but today she chose an ordinary dress—a pale blue with the most meager of trim—to accompany her father. The elaborate braiding of her hair was still in place, and in spite of a lack of effort on her part, her natural beauty radiated. Father and daughter both looked up with awe at the splendid Santa Suzanna as it loomed before them. Bianca had always found architecture fascinating, but the disappointment of the previous evening lingered.

"My good man, Stefano, and the beautiful Bianca Maria!" exclaimed Carlo Maderno, rushing down the front steps of the church to greet the two. Just behind him, with more deliberate steps, came one of his workmen, a tall, muscular youth with intense brown eyes. He stopped, hand on hip, with one foot on a step above the other.

Bianca involuntarily glanced toward the workman. When her eyes darted back for a second look, he seemed for a moment to be a heroic statue, in the stance of a Greek god— or no, maybe not.

"If you will forgive me," continued Carlo, "I find myself in the midst of solving an urgent construction problem. I will join you soon, but I have asked Marco Biliverti to discuss the façade with you. Marco is an excellent stonecutter, and, although he has been with me just a few weeks, he is not only talented in his trade, but I have made him a foreman. He seems to have a natural ability to direct others. You will find the young man most articulate. I give you Marco Biliverti. Signor Stefano Marinelli and the Signorina Bianca Maria." With this breathless introduction, Carlo leapt back up the steps and disappeared through the enormous open doorway.

For a moment time seemed frozen. Bianca now looked fully into his intriguing eyes. They seemed to pierce to her very soul.

As she stood there, stunned by emotions that she did not comprehend, Marco discussed the semiengaged columns, the effect of perspective, the figural sculpture, the preponderance of the vertical. "And in short," he continued, "Carlo has created an architecture that suggests an upward surge of energies."

"An upward surge of energies?" Bianca repeated softly to herself.

"Pardon me, I failed to hear your question, signorina." Marco again seemed to lock his eyes on hers, but this time she was sure the intensity came only from discussing a subject he felt passionate about.

"Oh, nothing, nothing at all. I–I was just admiring the structure."

Marco was dressed in the usual clothes of a workman: a simple wide-sleeved shirt and nondescript jerkin, cinched with a leather belt over coarse hosen. But his smooth-shaven face and his hair, short and tousled but lustrous, seemed better suited to a man of aristocratic origin. His deep, cultured voice and demeanor also belied this humble status.

". . .a harmonious interplay of light and shadows," she heard him saying.

At that moment Carlo Maderno returned in a more relaxed state. "I hope you have not been disappointed with Marco's discussion?" he began.

"Not in the least," Stefano answered enthusiastically. "On the contrary, he has shown himself to be most knowledgeable, and we find the façade extremely fascinating. Is that not so, Bianca Maria? I'm sure there will be even greater commissions in store for you."

"It was not for praise that I invited you here, though I

humbly thank you. You had told me of your daughter's avid interest in the new art projects of Rome. . .and also I have a business matter about which I wish to seek your advice. Could we perhaps step inside a few minutes? Perchance Bianca has further questions for Marco."

With that the two older men disappeared into the nave of the church, leaving the two young persons to delve more deeply into the elements of the new architecture—or whatever else they might choose to discuss.

Relaxing his posture, Marco turned to Bianca with an amiable smile. "Well, enough talking about rocks," he said.

"I was just wondering which 'rocks' were cut by your hands," said Bianca, glancing up at the building. The young man had put her at ease; thus, that frozen moment of insight faded as an illusion.

"You really are interested? I thought your father was merely showing his pride in you, as fathers are wont to do."

Bianca smiled shyly as Marco continued. "I cannot pick out which blocks show my handiwork, but I am responsible for the final carving of the two large scrolls on either side of the second story. Some critics are trying to debase Carlo's design by calling his work 'baroque.' "

"I find it expressive of the new Rome," said Bianca. "If I may be so bold as to ask, do you come from a family of stonecutters?"

"Actually, I was apprenticed to a stonecutter for two years as a boy. My father felt everyone should learn a trade. But, no, my people are wine growers from Terni."

"Then why. . .?"

"Why am I not home picking grapes?" Marco laughed. "It's a long and complex story, but suffice it to say that my father, having always been in robust health, died suddenly of severe pains in his chest—in the early part of this year's abundant harvest. When the season's business was finally complete, I brought my widowed mother and young sister to

Rome for a visit with my uncle's family, so that we could all rest and mourn among relatives. A dire turn of events has left us here with a greatly diminished manner of living."

"I offer you my condolences on the loss of your father. You must be very angry over your dire misfortune," said Bianca in all sincerity.

"No. I was briefly angry, but have learned to turn such emotions toward solving the immediate problems. In this case, I am cutting stone while mentally seeking a way. . .a way out of our dire circumstances. Actually, I rather enjoy the manual labor.

"But enough of my concerns. Tell me why a young lady like yourself is so fascinated with the new architecture," Marco said in a much lighter tone, turning his attentions entirely to her.

No one had ever asked her so directly about her opinions. Bianca bit her lip and searched her mind for a frivolous response that would guard her femininity. Finding none, she burst out with her true feelings: "I believe Rome is on the verge of again becoming the greatest city in the world. Construction is taking place all over. Fountains and statues are springing up everywhere. . . ."

"Like a veritable garden sprouting flowers in springtime," Marco inserted jokingly.

They both laughed over the image brought to mind of little buds rapidly growing into full-fledged fountains and statues. Bianca was afraid he was not taking her seriously and wished she had come up with a less intellectual response. But when he said, "Go on. I'm sorry to have interrupted," she found the courage to continue.

"It is really painting I feel most ardent about. I am especially enthralled with the tableaux of Michele Merisi da Caravaggio."

"Caravaggio? I met him at the Christian fellowship my family has been visiting—the followers of Filippo Neri, who meet at the recently constructed Chiesa Nuova. Perhaps you have heard of the group?"

"No, I regret that I haven't. But tell me what you know about. . .about the great Caravaggio," Bianca said, tripping over her words in excitement."

"Oh, is he great? All I know is that shortly after I met him, he came by here as I was working one day and asked me to model for a painting he is commissioned to do of St. John the Baptist. Apparently it is his habit to pick his models thus."

Bianca's jaw dropped in astonishment, but before she could learn more, Stefano and Carlo returned. The two men shook hands as if something had been settled. Pleasantries and good-byes were said all around. Marco returned to his work, and the Marinellis made their way back toward the Via Margutta.

Bianca was lost in thought, grappling with the feelings and questions left by this most pleasant meeting. The initial thrill of encountering Marco had left her acting like a speechless ninny, but once they were alone, his manner calmed her, made her feel as if she could share her heart's longings with him. What dire misfortune had befallen Marco's family? Why was the beating of her heart so quickened? What could this young man know, or what could he learn, about Caravaggio? Marco would be in the artist's studio. He would soon know how he worked, with how many assistants, apprentices. . .

"So Carlo Maderno has been offered the commission of enlarging St. Peter's," Stefano remarked as if to himself while the two strolled along. "He wants to discuss further with me some financial considerations."

"Then, Papa, we will return to Santa Suzanna?"

"Most unlikely," he responded, without perceiving the reason for her question. "The façade will be completed within a few weeks."

❧

For Marco's part, he returned to his chiseling, his head full of pleasant images of the lovely Bianca. He admired her poise, her acceptance of his humor, her knowledge and understanding of contemporary topics, the ease with which she spoke to him, and, of course, her natural, unassuming beauty. But he was in no position now to approach her as an equal.

He mulled over the catastrophic events of the past few weeks. His father's death had certainly been a tragic loss, but the dire circumstances that followed had turned his world upside down.

Marco had never really known his half brother Jacopo, who had left home in his teens when his widowed father married Costanza. During those early years, the father had pitied the motherless Jacopo and furnished him with a living allowance, which permitted him to go his own way. The young Costanza soon began a second family with the birth of Marco and, later, a daughter, Anabella.

As a fourth of the populace in Terni was now in the service of the Biliverti seigniory, in early summer the father had pleaded with Jacopo to return and learn about the cultivation and harvest of vineyards and the supervision of laborers. As the elder son, the father had always expected him to take over in his father's old age; a substantial stipend was to be provided for Marco, who had been destined for scientific studies at the University of Padua.

Jacopo's response to his father's plea had been to take, unauthorized, a large portion of the family fortune and squander it among his licentious friends in Madrid. He brought dishonor upon the Biliverti name with various sordid ventures. At this point the father called Marco home from his studies. Although regretting the turn of events, Marco nevertheless willingly relieved his father of many responsibilities.

Much to Marco's surprise, and, indeed, under his protest, the father sent a letter of "disinheritance with just cause" to the older son. He then wrote out his last will and testament, signed it, and gave it to Marco for safekeeping. His plan was to legally record it after the grape harvest. Alas, he waited too long.

Marco thought about what his life might have been had his father not died. He had already spent his twentieth year at the University of Padua, studying under the world renowned physicist Galileo Galilei. Galileo's inventions and discovery of the influence of gravity on heavenly bodies had been bitterly opposed, but Marco found his lectures captivating. The great teacher had even confided to Marco and a few other select students his ideas for constructing a device that would allow scientists to look into the universe and enlarge their view of the heavenly bodies—to more closely study them. Marco felt that to be a part of such discoveries would be the ultimate in life satisfaction.

The most vivid scene that came to Marco's mind, as he leveled a block of stone, had occurred after his father's funeral. His own consoling words were not enough to ease his mother's loss. At his suggestion, the family undertook the two-day carriage ride to Rome to spend some time in the comfort of her brother's family. He recalled the excitement of his eleven-year-old sister, Anabella, who had never visited the big city. How enjoyable it had been to see all the new monuments and old ruins so fresh through her wide eyes!

Then one night, just as the family was retiring, a servant from their castle in Terni arrived on horseback with a message: "Your half brother Jacopo has confiscated the castle and taken charge of the seigniory. You must come quickly if you are ever to claim what is yours."

Marco relived the long ride, begun that very evening. After spending the next night at an inn, he arrived at the castle in the morning. Rebuffed by a frightened servant girl at the door, he begged her pardon and, taking her firmly by the shoulders, pushed past her. He then ran upstairs to his bedroom, where he ripped open the secret wall panel. The will was missing!

The anger that Marco had so blithely denied to Bianca still lived on. It surged up in his breast now as he recalled confronting Jacopo on his return down the stairway.

"Where is our father's will, and why have you so dishonored his death?" he shouted.

"I am the elder by seventeen years, my dear Marco," Jacopo said with uncharacteristic calmness. "No court in the land would deny my right to this property as the elder son of an old, noble family. I am afraid there is nothing you can do. Therefore, please forsake my premises at once before I am forced to call my Spanish guards."

"But, Jacopo, please reconsider," he recalled himself saying. "Where are my mother and little Anabella to live? You haven't the remotest idea of how to run a vast seignoiry such as we have. I have given this very serious thought during my long ride: I offer you a generous stipend, the same percentage my father had once authorized for me, before your actions forced him to change the order of inheritance. Will you not. . ."

"Step aside, you fool," he scoffed.

Marco had turned back toward Jacopo at the doorway. "I vow you will not get away with this cruel theft! For the honor of our father and the comfort of my mother, *I shall return!*" he had declared just before the heavy door slammed in his face.

four

A persistent hope lingered in Bianca's heart that she might see Marco again. But it had been nearly two weeks, and, alas, Rome was a very large city, making a chance meeting close to impossible.

She positioned herself on a bench in the Piazza del Popolo, the public square not far from her family's villa, to observe people in their varied activities and to sketch. As usual, she had brought the servant, Albret, with her to carry her drawing board, parchment sheets, and box of charcoal sticks. A bright and serious boy, tall for his age, he enjoyed these outings as much as she. Since a woman alone in Rome was vulnerable to crime, Albret's presence ensured her protection.

The afternoon was pleasant, a bright sun casting shadows of the monuments and clipped shrubbery. A mother and daughter feeding pigeons captivated Bianca. Behind them rose the stately Egyptian obelisk. The mother sat in its shadow, holding a chunk of stale bread from which she tore pieces for her daughter.

Bianca was especially enthralled with the girl—she judged her to be between ten and twelve years old. Her casual, lilac-colored dress was like that worn by children of the old nobility: a square neck, cuffs trimmed in lace. A dark ribbon tied back her chestnut curls, which bounced from side to side with the child's movement. Her arms stretched outward and upward as she threw the crumbs high above her. The pigeons were happy to play her game and catch the offerings in midair.

Bianca attached a large square of parchment to her board and began to sketch. She wanted to capture the very essence of joy in this drawing. The round face formed easily under her charcoal stick—sparkling eyes and a full-lipped mouth, open in playful innocence. But the arms and hands were in constant motion, making them difficult to follow.

"Pardon me, *signora* and *signorina*, I am attempting to sketch. . ." Bianca began as she approached the two.

"Do let me see. . . . How very talented you are! The sketch is a remarkable likeness of Anabella. Doesn't it look like you, my dear?" the mother exclaimed in admiration of Bianca's work. "And you would like Anabella to please hold still so that you may capture the arms." The woman, perhaps in her early forties, had preserved her own beauty well—in spite of her short, rather stout stature. Beside her, Bianca noticed a large bag of what appeared to be small, rolled-up pieces of needlework.

"Exactly so. I am Bianca Marinelli and live not far from the square."

"And I am Costanza Biliverti from Terni, and this is my daughter, Anabella. We arrived only a few weeks ago, and this child is fascinated with everything about the big city."

"And what do you like most, Anabella?" Bianca managed to ask, though her mouth had gone dry when she realized that this just might be Marco's family.

"The gardens, the palaces, the fountains—it's all so beautiful. But there are so many beggars and sick people on the streets. Does no one care for them? In Terni, there are no beggars. Papa hires them to work the vineyards. Or rather, he did. . ." Anabella broke off in a saddened tone.

"I believe I may have but recently met your brother," exclaimed Bianca. "Isn't he a stonecutter at the Santa Suzanna?"

"Yes, that is true. How surprising to meet by chance someone who knows him. Marco is such a good son, sacrificing so much for his family," exclaimed Costanza.

Bianca drew in her breath, hoping the woman would go on with some enlightening details, and so she did.

"I presume he told you how he was forced to give up his

studies at the University of Padua to help supervise the harvest. Then my husband died. He was doing so well with his scientific pursuits. . . . But he is most resourceful, always finding the good in every situation. He takes such excellent care of me and his sister. But we don't wish to detain you with all that. How would you like Anabella to pose?"

"First, my condolences on the loss of your husband," said Bianca. Then after a pause, "Anabella, just throw the morsels of bread into the air as you were doing, but keep your hands up for a few moments."

"Like this?" Anabella said, happy to oblige.

"Perfect. Just a few more seconds. . ." Bianca's charcoal stick flew across the page. She was fully aware that if she were a *real* artist in a studio, she would be forbidden, as a woman, to draw from a live model, even a child. "That's it. Thank you so very much."

"I'm a model like Marco is going to be!" said Anabella, flattered by the attention.

"Hush, child," whispered Costanza, embarrassed that her son had taken on such a lowly job.

Bianca decided to remain discreet on the topic of Marco. Noticing the lengthening shadows, she abruptly said, "I must be going. Mother will be worried. It has been so delightful meeting you. I hope to see you again."

"We come here quite often, but now that Santa Suzanna is almost finished. . .well, who knows. . . . It has been a pleasure meeting you, also. You are such a capable artist. Do you plan to do a painting from this sketch?"

"Yes, actually I do," said Bianca, surprised at her own words. She didn't even know how to grind and mix paints, much less wield a brush! Albret appeared suddenly beside her, taking her supplies, and they were gone.

❧

At that very moment Marco stood inside the church next to the square. Tomorrow would be his first sitting as a model.

He had been given no instructions other than, "Just come by after work and don't bother to freshen up." In one of the chapels hung two Caravaggio paintings, one of St. Paul's conversion and the other of St. Peter. He had come here to study the poses of the figures to gain some insight into how the artist worked. He found both quite moving without knowing why. So Caravaggio is a *great* painter. At least Bianca had thought so. He wished she were beside him now to elaborate on his style. In fact, he simply wished she were beside him.

Marco emerged from the church, spotted his mother and sister by the obelisk, and hurried to meet them. They had spent the day selling their embroidery in the marketplace. Often they would meet Marco here at the Piazza del Popolo as he returned from work.

"Marco, Marco, I'm a model like you," shouted Anabella as soon as she saw her brother.

Marco bent to kiss both mother and sister on the cheek. "What on earth are you chattering about, my little goose?" he said affectionately.

"We met a charming, young lady this afternoon, Bianca Marinelli, who wanted to sketch Anabella feeding the pigeons," Costanza explained. "She says she met you at the Santa Suzanna. How can that be? She appears to be of the new aristocracy of the merchant-banker class."

"And she's *pretty*, too, Marco," cut in Anabella.

"Yes, I did meet her. And yes, 'Bella, she is pretty," said Marco in total agreement. "The architect asked me to show her father and her the stone work on the front of the building. I think he is associated with a branch of the Medici bank here in Rome."

"I was on the verge of asking if she would like to wait until you arrived, but she seemed to be in a hurry and rushed off."

"Mother, you forget I am not a *marchese* at the moment. My class cannot mingle with hers." Conversation then turned to other topics as the family continued their walk home.

Costanza's benevolent brother had insisted that the ousted Bilivertis stay with his family until the castle was recovered. But Costanza soon began to feel that they were imposing. Her brother had already introduced them to the fellowship at Chiesa Nuova. There they found a group of sincere believers who welcomed them with the love of Christ Jesus.

The leaders, they found, taught everyone the Scriptures, believing that all who follow Jesus should be ministers to each other. They took little note of class distinctions and served all alike, visiting the sick, those in prison, and ministering to the poor and forgotten. Of most importance, the group met often for prayer and devotions, comforting and encouraging one another. As the now deceased founder, Filippo Neri, had been a lifelong friend of a high-ranking church official, they were left undisturbed to worship in such an unconventional manner.

Costanza felt a renewing of her spirit that eased the pain of her grieving heart. Realizing that pride of position is not pleasing to God, she became thankful for the worldly goods they did have and learned to rely on God to provide the rest. As part of a noblewoman's training, she had long ago learned to embroider and had been teaching her daughter the same. Now they went unashamed to the marketplace to sell their scarves, borders, and other such pieces of decorated cloth. It was not unpleasant and brought in a few *scudi* to help with expenses.

A gentleman of the fellowship owned several townhouses and offered the family one to rent at a fair price. The quarters were meager compared to the castle, but so far they had been able to keep with them the one servant brought from Terni. There was room for Marco's favorite horse in the stables, but they had had to sell the family carriage.

❧

The evening meal of rich soup, bread, and fruit had been prepared by the servant, who joined them at the crowded table—a habit the exiled family had insisted upon.

Marco blessed the food in a sincere prayer of thanksgiving, such as those he had heard at the fellowship.

Anabella chattered away about events at the market. For the benefit of the servant, she related for the second time how a thief, not more than seven years old, had slipped through the crowd, robbing several people before seeming to disappear into thin air. "I saw him moving quickly but couldn't tell what he was up to until someone yelled, 'I've been robbed!' "

" 'Bella, dear, I wish you didn't have to work in the market," said Marco.

"Oh, it's fun, Marco. Exciting things happen all the time," she responded with enthusiasm. "I don't mind at all." But then in a sadder tone she added, "What I do mind is losing our status. You will never find a nobleman for me to marry. I'll be a spinster for sure. And I refuse to be put in a convent."

"You have lots of time, my child. Don't be so eager," said the servant woman as she sliced the bread.

After a few quiet moments, Costanza broached the subject continually on all their minds. "Marco, I know how concerned you are over our financial welfare. What do you have, a couple of weeks more at Santa Suzanna?"

"Yes, Mother. There is the modeling job, but I doubt that it will pay much, though I understand that Caravaggio is a great painter—which suggests accompanying wealth.

"But of greater importance," continued Marco, "I have received a sealed message, brought by travelers from Terni, indicating that Jacopo has spread malicious and untrue tales about us in the village. Evidently he is trying to undermine me to gain support for himself in Terni. The message was unsigned, but the script looks like that of one of our trusted overseers. Additionally, it said that Jacopo has enlisted the aid of Bishop Mariano to support his ownership of the property. Short of possessing the title-deed along with my father's signed will, our best hope lies in finding an ally of high standing. Law, it seems, depends largely on the parties with whom one has connections."

"Bishop Mariano has oft befriended your father in the past. He would not, however, be privy to his more recent wishes—the change in his will. Jacopo is no doubt preying upon his sympathies. . . ."

"Most of my father's allies are no longer living. I know of no one in a position. . ."

"Let me present this idea," said Costanza, having thoughtfully formed a plan. "Our connection with the Marinelli family is most tenuous, but you did meet the father. Did you not say he was a banker with the Medicis? Perhaps he can suggest someone who feels strongly about the issue of rightful title-deeds. The controversy over verification of ownership only a few years ago caused many in high places to take a stand on one side or the other."

"Your suggestion is well taken, Mother. It is not a task I relish, but this is no time for timidity. I will give it some honest thought."

five

Marco arrived in front of the Palazzo Madama, ill at ease in his work clothes, having sweat a good deal from his walk in the warm sun from Santa Suzanna. It was a striking palace indeed, owned by the Grand Duke of Tuscany, who had loaned it to the Cardinal del Monte, who in turn had given the cellar studio to Caravaggio. Perhaps he would be refused entrance, but the artist had told him not to wash; he was to come directly from his work. He need not have had such fears. A guard met him at the gates and asked if he had come to model for Caravaggio. That confirmed, he was led through a side entrance, past multiple kitchens, to his destination.

"Buona sera, my good man," Caravaggio welcomed him enthusiastically. "The canvas is prepared and only awaits your good form."

"You are indeed a great man if you can work a miracle and turn my image into anything resembling John the Baptist."

"Do not worry. Don't you know that John stayed in the wilderness, eating locusts and wild honey? He could not possibly have lived in the polished body portrayed in most saintly pictures of the man. He was a real flesh-and-blood person, cousin of our Lord and Savior, yes; but he also was a man who was weighed down by the sorrows of mankind. Do you understand that, Marco?"

"Yes, I do. I understand that he lived and died for Jesus Christ. And for that reason I do not feel worthy to represent him."

"Well, we shall see. I will pay you more than you are worth on a daily basis. But if I cannot elicit from you the Baptist my painting needs—*arrividerci.* The streets of Rome are lined with the deposed sons of the old nobility!"

"I promise to give you my best," Marco said, feeling somewhat intimidated.

"Now, if you will just go behind that screen, disrobe completely and wrap the camel skin around your loins, then drape this crimson mantle about your shoulders, we shall begin."

Marco did as he was instructed and soon emerged, draped and barefoot, feeling even more foolish than he had at the gate. He sat on the indicated low bench and held the simple reed cross given him. Without a word, the artist took a great deal of time arranging and rearranging the folds of the mantle. When at last he seemed satisfied, he stepped back on the other side of the easel.

After selecting a stylus, he began rapidly to etch the principal lines of the composition into the layers of undercoat he had prepared on the large canvas. "Now, you may be at ease while I adjust the light, but remain seated," the artist directed.

Out of the corner of his eye Marco could tell that Caravaggio was lighting a lantern. After leaning a flimsy ladder against the wall, he climbed up and hung the lamp next to a high window, thus creating a raking light across Marco's body.

"I thought I—rather, St. John—was in the wilderness," said Marco.

"You are."

"The sun?" Marco said, pointing to the lantern.

"No. The true Light of the World."

"Jesus Christ?"

"Yes."

With that brief explanation, Caravaggio again arranged the mantle around Marco so that the shadows fell to his satisfaction. He donned an overblouse and began mixing paint, stirring furiously. Marco thought this must be the easiest work in the world—to just sit. He looked around the large, bare room and realized this was the artist's entire living quarters.

There was only the single window, an unmade bed, a French armoire, a cluttered desk with a wide shelf of books, many costumes for props, and, he assumed, access to the palace kitchens.

Caravaggio was clean-shaven like himself and probably only a few years older. Though rumpled, he was finely dressed in the fashion of the day—in black, padded doublet and trunk hosen. His black cape lay over the back of the only chair in the room.

After perhaps thirty minutes at the canvas, Caravaggio's booming voice broke the tension of silence. "Well done. I am pleased. Now, I must mix up some more paints, and we shall chat a bit. You may relax."

"If I may ask, is it the Cardinal del Monte who has commissioned this work?" queried Marco, mostly to get some conversation going, now that he had permission to speak.

"No, this is for a small oratory in the Costa fiefdom of Conscente. It is being commissioned by Ottavio Costa, the state banker. But it was the cardinal who commissioned the three paintings of St. Matthew that now hang in San Luigi dei Francesi, adjacent to the Palazzo. You have, no doubt, seen these masterpieces?"

Marco admitted that he had not.

Caravaggio began to dab paint on the canvas. "Are you a part of the fellowship that meets at Chiesa Nuova?" the artist asked in a more pleasant voice, recalling their first meeting there.

As the two were alone in the studio, Marco felt at ease to discuss his religious life. "Yes. Those wonderful people have been most helpful to my family. My mother especially has been much comforted. She and my young sister have been visiting a hospital with a small group from the fellowship. I believe such activity has helped ease their adjustment to this different life. And as for myself, I have found a new meaning of spirituality. They have made the Scriptures understandable for me."

"I see. Shortly after I arrived in Rome, penniless, with nothing but my paints and a few rolls of canvas, someone told me to go to the Chiesa Nuova," countered Caravaggio with a similar story. "This was in 1592, three years before Filippo Neri died. I went seeking charity, but received solace for my anguished spirit as well.

"Neri gave me more than an hour of his time, and I absorbed and believed every word he said. He made the Word of God come to life and speak to my troubled soul. He said everyone does wrong, but God stands ready to forgive when we ask Him. Since that meeting, I have yearned for nothing more than to make the Scriptures meaningful and understandable to the common man. That is why I must always work with models I find on the streets—people who have known suffering. Now if you will get back into position. . . ," Caravaggio said in a tone that let Marco know it was time to be silent again.

The monotonous brush strokes, interspersed with an occasional "humph" from the artist, nearly put Marco to sleep. His head began to nod.

"That's it!" shouted Caravaggio. "Hold you head just like that." The room grew still again for what must have been at least thirty minutes. Then suddenly, "No, no, that will never do!" He groaned and threw his paint cloth on the floor.

Not knowing what to make of this outburst, Marco remained in position. Soon he heard the swish of a brush again. "Fine, fine. Very fine," he heard the master mutter.

After perhaps another thirty minutes, Caravaggio abruptly handed Marco a handful of gold *scudi* and said with a defeated demeanor, "Come back the same time tomorrow. I will try again."

Marco quietly let himself out, leaving the artist with his overblouse drawn up over his face.

❧

The following day, as Marco approached the Palazzo Madama,

he noticed for the first time the church of the San Luigi dei Francesi. *Ah yes, the St. Matthew masterpieces that Caravaggio mentioned,* Marco thought. *I must have a look.* The church was empty except for a young woman, kneeling in prayer. Marco felt the need of a short talk with God before assuming the persona of St. John the Baptist. He knelt and bowed his head.

As he rose to look for the paintings, the young woman turned to leave. Their eyes met.

"Bianca, what a surprise to find you here. Is it not unsafe for you to be alone?"

"Albret, our trusted servant, is just outside. I came to sketch the fountains of the Piazza Navona," Bianca said, somewhat defensively. "This is my family's church, and I feel it is my duty to say a prayer when I am close by. And what brings you here?"

"I'm on my way for my second sitting for the great Caravaggio, who lives in the Palazzo Madama over there," he said with a flourish of his arm in the direction of the palace. "I would be most pleased to see some of your draw. . ."

"Caravaggio lives there? And this is where you come to model?" Bianca exclaimed, her face glowing with enthusiasm. "How very fortunate you are!"

"Well, perhaps," said Marco, realizing that the glow of enthusiasm was for Caravaggio, not for himself. He became suddenly aware of his shabby clothes and odor of sweat from an honest day's work. Inside, he still thought of himself as the son of the Marchese of Terni, a comfortable role he had enjoyed all his life. But to Bianca—bright as sunshine in her pale yellow dress—he knew he was a common laborer. "I must be going. I don't want to keep the 'great' man waiting," he said without an audible note of sarcasm.

"Yes, of course."

The two stood facing each other for several uneasy seconds. Then together they turned from the quiet of the sanctuary and walked out into the sounds of splashing fountains, muting the cacophony of the Roman street.

"I didn't see any Caravaggio paintings," Marco mentioned before bidding her good-bye.

"Oh, they're in a private chapel," Bianca said. Then with an inviting smile, she added, "Perhaps I could show them to you someday."

Bianca spotted Albret pitching pebbles into the Fountain of Neptune while he waited for her. Watching Marco walk toward the palace, she felt a thrill of excitement—to be so near Caravaggio.

Or was it in being near Marco? He was so pleasant and thoughtful—and easy to talk with. Not at all like the stuffy men she usually encountered. So his family had a little vineyard in Terni. Dire circumstances had diminished their manner of living, she surmised, perhaps through mismanagement. They must have had *some* money or he couldn't have been a student at the university. They probably had done well in a few grape harvests. *If only he were of a higher social level—and if only he would wash his hands and face before entering church.*

six

A nervous, young gentleman in noble attire rang the bell at the Marinelli gate. His ample black cloak was pulled across his body and thrown back over his left shoulder in the new fashion of the day. His lustrous short hair was well groomed, and he carried a pair of leather gloves in his right hand.

A slender, well-groomed youth with a bit of fuzz beginning to show on his chin quickly arrived. Without any attempt to use the large key dangling from his belt, he pleasantly inquired, "Good afternoon, *signore*. May I ask your name and purpose in calling?"

"I am the Marchese Marco Biliverti of Terni come to discuss a business—rather a private—matter with Signor Marinelli. Please tell him I regret calling on a Sunday, but I did not know the location of his business—that is if he is home at this hour."

"Is he expecting you?" said the youth, Albret by name.

"No. He is not." Marco hesitated, then continued, "Please suggest to him that he may remember our meeting at the Santa Suzanna a couple of weeks ago."

Uncomfortable at leaving a *marchese* waiting at the gate, Albret turned the large key in the lock, saying, "Since Signor Marinelli knows you, I'm sure he would want you to wait inside."

Following Albret across the flagstone pathway that led to the villa entrance, Marco noticed the well-kept grounds; a small fountain with statues of frolicking dolphins; and the simple, though elegant, exterior that recalled a style of the early Renaissance.

Once inside, Albret said, "You may wait here while I inform Signor Marinelli of your presence." He indicated a high-backed

39

chair. Marco took the seat and surveyed the mixture of French and Italian furnishings, the tapestries on the walls, and a single marble statue of a Roman youth, draped in a loose toga. Off to the side of the sitting room, Marco noticed double doors that opened to a small family chapel. Sunlight streamed through the one stained-glass window.

Mentally, Marco rehearsed his purpose for being here, along with the choices of requests he might make—according to how his story would be received.

"Good afternoon, Marchese Biliberti," Stefano said politely, though rather stiffly. "My servant tells me we have met, though I don't recall. . ."

Marco stood and offered his hand, which the older man clasped formally. "Biliverti, with a 'v,' " he corrected. "It was at the church of Santa Suzanna. Your daughter was with you. In the absence of the architect, Carlo Maderno, I. . ."

"Ah, yes, I do recall. You are the articulate stonemason. *Marchese* it is then? The Marchese Marco Biliverti? I regret that I did not recognize you," Stefano said with a hint of warmth. "And you have a matter you wish to discuss with me?"

Marco felt the conversation had not gotten off to a good start, but nevertheless he plunged ahead. Being as straightforward and honest as possible, he recounted the whole sad story of how his half brother Jacopo had confiscated the family seignoiry against the will of his late father. "As of course you are aware, legal recourse in our country rests largely with the influence of those in powerful positions. The police take care of petty theft and the like, but this. . ."

Stefano, who until this point had sat nodding to indicate he was following the story, suddenly interrupted. "True. We all know the unfair conditions we live under, but I have made a great effort throughout my life to conform to accepted practices of the day. If they change, I change. I live and let live. Peace at all cost. Thus I have been able to get ahead in this world, to rise to a certain financial level whereby I can provide security for my wife and children—who mean more to me than life itself. I have only two children now; my dear eldest son spoke out against some business practices that he felt were unfair. For his trouble he was murdered by thugs of the Spanish empire hardly three months ago."

"I am sorry to hear. . ."

"I should not have mentioned that. My wife and daughter think he was killed randomly by bandits," confided Stefano. "My other son, Reginoldo, is in Florence studying law—also a precarious endeavor. At any rate, I simply cannot become involved in the misfortunes of others. You seem like a bright and deserving young man, but I hope you will understand that I cannot bring any more danger to my family. I love them too much." With that Stefano stood and extended his hand, indicating the discussion was over.

"I understand perfectly," said Marco, rising but declining the outstretched hand. "However, the favor I have come to request should not in any way put yourself or your family at risk. Would you be so kind as to hear me out?"

Stefano nodded, and both men sat down. Mentally Marco shifted to a less aggressive request than he had hoped to make. "The controversy over verification of ownership only a few years ago left many feeling strongly one way or the other," he began in a confident voice, remembering his mother's words. "I merely wish to gain from you a few names of those who might be sympathetic to my cause. It is a just cause. Like yourself, I deeply love my family—my widowed mother and sister—and feel responsible for their welfare. My father had many fine connections in Terni and in Rome. The most influential of those have died.

"As for myself, I was away at the University of Padua and never expected to be in charge of our large seigniory. That was to be my elder brother's role. When our father disinherited him for just cause, the responsibility fell to me. Jacopo has enlisted the help of Bishop Mariano, who had often befriended my father in the past. The bishop believes an estate should always go to the eldest son and that he alone should be left to share as he chooses. Jacopo has no intention of providing for even my mother and sister."

Just at that crucial moment, Bianca entered with a tray of refreshing drinks. "Excuse me, Papa, but Albret told me you had a visitor. May I pour you each. . ." Suddenly she recognized that face, those deep brown eyes turned toward her. ". . .a drink?"

"Yes, Bianca Maria. That is most thoughtful of you. Please pour a goblet for our friend, the Marchese of Terni. Perhaps you remember his excellent commentary on the architecture of Santa Suzanna?"

"Marchese?" she said, startled for a second time in two minutes. "I mean, Marchese, how pleasant to see you again. Here's a goblet for you. And one for you, Papa. Now, if you will excuse me, I will leave you to continue your discussion."

"I believe we have finished with business, my dear," Stefano said, happy to find an escape for the moment from the subject just presented to him. "Please take the chair between us." Turning to Marco, he asked, "And has the Santa Suzanna been completed?"

"Actually, it has. But there remain several more days of removing debris. I have been asked to stay on as a foreman of the crew."

"Then perhaps you will be asked to work on the enlargement of St. Peter's Basilica?" said Stefano.

"Perhaps. I believe that Carlo Maderno has been appointed architect, but it will, no doubt, take a year or so to draw up the plans."

Avoiding any reference to his modeling, Bianca took this opportunity to boldly ask Marco, "Marchese, I understand you are a friend of the artist, Caravaggio. Have you ever had an opportunity to visit his studio, to watch him work?"

"Yes, *signorina,* I have. He doesn't even sketch his composition in advance, but using a stylus, quickly traces the major lines directly onto his canvas."

"Amazing," said Stefano.

"Such a famous artist, no doubt, has many apprentices working in his shop," Bianca ventured.

Marco chuckled, recalling recent scenes at the studio. "No, he works alone. That man is too ill-tempered to have even one apprentice. It's a wonder he can get poor devils from the street to model for him," he said in an off-handed sort of way, totally unaware of the effect such a comment would have on Bianca.

"Excuse me, Papa, I am not feeling well," Bianca said, rushing from the room to conceal her tears. She had waited for the perfect moment to present the idea of an apprenticeship to her father. This had seemed the perfect opening. Now, all her hopes and dreams had been crushed. *Caravaggio doesn't even have apprentices! But surely Marco was joking about his temper,* thought Bianca as she buried her head in a pillow and let the tears flow.

❧

"Perhaps I misspoke," said Marco, shifting in his chair. "I certainly would not want to offend your daughter."

"I believe she was just not feeling well," said Stefano, who always found himself at a loss when either his wife or daughter became upset. He stood, making a second attempt to dismiss the challenge before him.

Marco followed his cue and stood. "It is not easy for me to make a request such as I have, *signore.* Especially of someone I have only recently met."

The older man appeared deep in thought, then said, "Marco—if I may call you Marco—you have made a good case, and I find your cause worthy. I don't know why—perhaps in honor of my lost son—but I would like to help you. Let me again make it clear that I must avoid at all costs bringing harm to my loved ones. Names do not come immediately to mind, but I will think on it. Any information must be passed verbally. I do not want names nor information to be written."

"Thank you. I understand."

"I cannot promise that I will come up with an appropriate influential person. But I believe it would be best if we met here. Would next Sunday afternoon, following siesta, be a good time for you?" Stefano was surprised at himself for making such a bold and generous offer.

"Yes, that would be very satisfactory," Marco said, trying to conceal his joy as the two shook hands and parted.

ஓ

Meanwhile, Bianca beat her fists into her pillow, then wiped her eyes with a handkerchief and tried to take stock of the situation. The anger was directed toward Marco. But why? Surely it was not his fault that Caravaggio did not take apprentices. Perhaps the anger was due to his casual, light-hearted attitude toward a subject very serious to her. *And what is he doing coming to this house dressed up like a marchese and putting on airs,* she thought. *What does he want from Papa? Money, no doubt.* A plan of action began to form in her mind.

seven

Bianca and Albret arrived at Santa Suzanna in midmorning. The overcast sky and chill in the air reflected Bianca's mood. Anticipating the cold, marble steps, she had brought a thin cushion to sit on. She pulled her ample wool kerchief around her shoulders, reached out for her drawing sheets from Albret, and settled into position. Marco would, no doubt, pass by at some point, and she could innocently claim her sole purpose in coming was to sketch the old olive trees across from the church.

Albret took his cue to wander the environs nearby, his short, unadorned dagger swinging visibly at his side. He took the responsibility of guarding his charge seriously—though, never having been challenged, his mind easily wandered.

A short distance away, workmen were piling chunks of stone and other debris onto a wagon tied behind two sleeping mules. Another crew was raking smooth the dirt surrounding the edifice. Bianca began a sketch of an ancient, twisted olive tree. The anger she had brought with her began to subside. Drawing had a way of calming her spirit. The monotonous scraping of the rakes faded as Bianca became totally absorbed in her work—unaware of shadowy figures drawing closely behind her.

Suddenly shouts of "*Signorina,* watch out!" brought her back to the real world. Startled, she stood up, causing her sketch board to go tumbling down the steps. Shock and fear immobilized her—a dagger and a rapier, spelling danger on either side. The dagger she quickly realized was Albret's. The rapier was in the hand of Marco! The situation clarified further as her eyes followed two men who dashed past the rudely awakened mules and disappeared into the bushes beyond.

Marco was first to speak. "Bianca! I didn't know it was you—in danger."

"Bianca, I'm so sorry," bemoaned Albret, rubbing his youthfully tanned face. "I only looked away a few moments. If I'd only been more alert, I could have carved them both up!"

"I–I don't even know what happened," said Bianca, still shaking with fright.

"Bianca, both men were standing behind you, each ready to grab an arm. They would have covered your face and dragged you off into those bushes. . . . I'm so happy you were not hurt," said Marco, sheathing his rapier.

"One had a rock in his hand to knock you over the head," said Albret. "Wish I'd run him through and through!"

A small crowd was gathering—passersby and workmen. "Back to work, men," ordered Marco. "The lady fortunately is unharmed." Their mumbling, as they drifted away, indicated a disappointment that the entertainment had not been greater.

Marco picked up the sketch board, scattered sheets of parchment, and the cushion. "Come inside, Bianca, where it is more secure. And Albret, would you like to stand guard in case they return?"

Albret was proud to do so. In fact, he longed to turn his momentary negligence into heroism.

Inside, the church was bare except for some mannerist frescos on the walls, a stark altar, and a long, wooden bench left by workmen. Services would not begin for another month.

"Bianca, are you all right?"

"Yes, I think so," she said weakly.

"I know you are a strong woman, independent and adventurous. I admire that, Bianca. But you must be more careful. Rome has an evil side lurking beneath its beauty."

"I know, Marco. Only this past year has Papa let me venture out to sketch. He has trained Albret in the art of defense and feels he is now skilled enough to protect me. Papa thinks I only go to the Piazza del Popolo, where I met your mother and sister, but I have always felt safe when venturing elsewhere, too," she said. "Papa would die if anything happened to me."

"I'm sure of it," said Marco, remembering her father's words about what his family meant to him.

"Bianca, shall we thank God right here and now for his protection?"

"Of course." They knelt on the stone floor.

"Father God," prayed Marco, "we know you are always with us. We feel your love surrounding us now as we humbly bow before you. We thank you from the depth of our souls for protecting Bianca from the evil that just now approached her. Give us the strength and courage to love others as you have loved us. In the name of our Lord Jesus Christ we pray. Amen."

As they rose, Marco noticed that tears were streaking down Bianca's face. "You are still frightened, aren't you, Bianca?" he said. "Let's go sit over there. He touched her lightly on the elbow and directed her toward the bench along the wall.

When they were seated, Bianca wiped her face with her handkerchief and said, "No, Marco, I am not still frightened. . . . I–I have never heard anyone pray like that. All I know are the prayers I have been taught. I pray mostly because I'm afraid not to. My parents have taught me to do everything the church says for us to do. . .and I try, but God always seems so far away. Just now as you prayed, I felt God's love around us, just as you said."

"That's good," said Marco.

"Marco, thank you. If you hadn't been there. . ."

"Then Albret would have had to run them through and

through." They both laughed.

"Marco, since we are in church I have a confession to make—to you. I came here today with a plan to confront you. It's silly, but somehow I was angry at you because you were the one who told me Caravaggio didn't take apprentices—and because you said he was ill-tempered. I also was determined to make you confess why you came to see my father dressed like a marchese."

"Well, I. . ."

"No, Marco, I am no longer angry. And the other. . .is none of my business. I just felt like confessing how foolish I had been."

"And maybe I would like to do a little confessing, too. As soon as I made that thoughtless statement about your artist friend being ill-tempered, I knew I had upset you. So I'm sorry. Actually, Caravaggio is a very spiritual man. He tries to show in his paintings that ordinary people can be transformed, if they let the light of God into their lives. Would you like to know how he makes figures burst out of the shadows into the light on his canvas?"

"More than anything!"

Marco noticed that Caravaggio glow pass across her face again, but he suppressed his jealousy and bravely continued. "He hangs a lantern up high on the wall."

"That is so fantastically clever!"

"He's not the only clever artist in Rome," said Marco. "Look at your sketch of this twisted olive tree. The limbs reach right out at you from the surface of the parchment. How do you make it so real?"

"That's one of Caravaggio's techniques. I study his paintings. But when he adds the light, the oil paint, the rich colors, it is really extraordinary," said Bianca. "Do you really think my sketch is good?"

"Yes, I do. I think your father should hire a tutor to give you painting lessons."

"Do you?" said Bianca, encouraged. "But both my parents believe the only life for a woman is to marry. They are eager to pledge me to a son of the old—and still prosperous—nobility. You know, many of these families have lost their lands. If it were up to me, I would never marry," she added resolutely.

"You think marriage would mean giving up painting?"

"Yes. My mother wanted to be a composer of music. Everyone thought it was a nice amusement for a young, unmarried woman. But they all, including my father, scoffed at the idea after she married. I was betrothed once—to Roland. I was only fourteen, and it frightened me so. I felt as if I had been sentenced to prison. It was a terrible, suffocating sensation. I hardly knew him, but I cried and wore black when he died of the plague. I was truly sorry, but—it sounds terrible to admit—I felt I had my life back."

"You've never known love then?"

"I love my parents and my brothers. I am still mourning my older brother's recent death. I think it was an official murder by the Spanish empire, but my parents refuse to discuss it. I adore my brother Reginoldo. He is a good man. . . . To answer your question, no, I've never been in love with a man."

"Bianca, I must get back to supervising the workers. Have you recovered sufficiently to go straight home with Albret?" Marco said abruptly.

"Yes, Marco, I'm fine. But I've babbled on about my life. . . ."

"Please don't make apologies. I am to meet with your father again on Sunday. Will you be there to serve refreshments?" he said, his eyes smiling.

She assured him she would be. Albret whisked her away at the door, and Marco was left with a longing in his heart—for the fair lady he had just rescued but could not pursue.

❧

The overcast sky brought forth a downpour, soaking Bianca and Albret as they rushed back to the villa. A key from

Albret's belt let them in a side door. Bianca was relieved that neither of her parents was at home. "Albret, please don't mention to Papa or Mother the little incident at Santa Suzanna. You know we should not have been there," cautioned Bianca, taking leave of the boy at the bottom of the staircase.

Once in her room, she quickly dried off and changed into a more comfortable chamber robe. She shook from the chill, but the trembling inside was a mixture of fright and emotion. She picked up some needlework, begun several days before, and sat by the French doors, which yielded the best light.

An hour passed. Then tapping on the bedroom door startled her, until she heard, "It's me, Sylvia. May I come in?"

Eagerly Bianca unlatched the door. She needed a talk with an old friend.

"Are you all right, Bianca?" Sylvia inquired. "I saw the two of you duck in the side door out of this horrid rain. May the Lord have mercy, so that we don't have as bad a rainy season as in the last year. All that mud! Albret can drive the covered carriage, you know. Even though you go only to the nearby piazza, when it's threatening like this. . . Well, you could be sick from the chill. Here, I brought you a hot herb drink." She set the tray down on a small table beside Bianca and poured a cup.

Sylvia stood, hands on hips, waiting to hear that her charge was in good shape so that Sylvia could be about her other chores.

"Sylvia, thank you. You are a good woman," said Bianca, still shaking. "It's not the outside chill. It's the turmoil churning inside that I need to talk about. Please sit down."

"My dear child," said Sylvia, pulling up a stool near Bianca. "What is it?"

"Men."

"Men? That's always the trouble!" Sylvia laughed, relieved that it was not a more serious matter.

Bianca chuckled a bit in agreement, then became somber

again. "Do you remember that when I was betrothed to Roland, Mother told me all the facts, the physical things—what to expect, how to take care of myself, and so on. It scared me half to death. Then you told me all about love, what real love between a man and a woman was meant to be. I was more scared after that than. . ."

"Yes, I recall our little talks. You said you didn't have that kind of love for Roland. And I told you about my wonderful husband, who had perished in a skirmish with some scoundrels. Our marriage had *also* been arranged, as most are, but I grew to love him more than my own life. That wonderful, intimate kind of love, blessed by God, is possible, Bianca."

"But Sylvia, I don't ever want to be married," she said, biting her lower lip and tightening her fists. "Is that wrong?"

"No, it's not wrong. But how would you live? Be realistic. Your parents will not always be here for you. Reginoldo will inherit this villa eventually."

"Listen, Sylvia. If I didn't marry, I would have my dowry. If Papa would only allow me to have painting lessons. . . This is the time to be an artist in Rome. The style is changing. The churches and public buildings, the old nobility and the new merchant-banker class—all are seeking paintings. The great artists cannot keep up with their commissions. I want to rise to the top, Sylvia. I want to paint like Caravaggio. I think sometimes I *love* Caravaggio. Is that possible, Sylvia? Can you love someone you haven't even seen?"

"I don't know, Bianca, but I doubt it."

"My feelings, then, are very confusing. If I had a husband. . .if I did, I would want to feel about him like I feel about Caravaggio. When I see his tremendous insight into the human soul in his paintings, I just know he must be a beautiful person inside. He would let me paint if I were his wife, because he would understand my passion for art. We could paint together. He could teach me his secrets. He would. . ."

"Bianca, poor Bianca. . . ," soothed Sylvia, realizing her charge had created a make-believe situation.

"Then, Sylvia, there is this other man, Marco Biliverti, who is a stonecutter. He is such a wonderfully good friend. I was thrilled the first time I looked into his eyes. I'm happy every minute I am with him, but the awe and mystery that I feel when I think of Caravaggio is missing. Now, if I could put together in one man the talent, mystery, and insight of a Caravaggio, the sincere spirit and humor of a Marco, and add the kiss of a Roland—then perhaps marriage would not be such a bad prospect."

"You must be realistic, Bianca. The two living ones are not of your class, which makes marriage to either impossible. Trust your parents to find you a good match. A perfect man does not exist—nor a perfect woman, either. But it is possible for true love to see beyond the imperfections."

"But if I *have* to marry, I must have it all to make up for the loss, Sylvia. I know it's a fantasy, but I want nothing less. Anything less would crush my spirit and make me forever bitter—like Mother. But why must I be forced to marry? God gave me a talent. Don't you think He wants me to use it for His glory?"

"I don't know. . . ."

Bianca stared at a large, carved chest that sat across from her. "That horrible *cassone,* full to the brim with trousseau, sits here in my room, reminding me day and night that I must be betrothed. I hate it. It's a symbol of a tomb to me."

"It was a gift from Roland, was it not?"

"Yes, that was sweet of him. But he never knew how I viewed marriage. He left the front panel for Papa to find an artist to paint a scene that would please me. I would never agree to anything he suggested—he thought the story of Ruth and Boaz would be wonderful. Finally I told him I would paint it myself. And I would, if I could just have some lessons."

"Poor Bianca, you do have a stubborn, unyielding mind."

"Yes, I most certainly do. I must follow my dream, Sylvia. I am resolved to ask Papa to find a lesser artist to tutor me in the use of oil paint. Then I can go and study Caravaggio's paintings in the churches and public places. In a way, he will still be my primary tutor. I know of other excellent artists who do this. Oh, thank you—thank you, Sylvia."

"Any time, my dear," Sylvia said, picking up the tray and knowing full well that Bianca had come to her own conclusion. "You had better dress for dinner now. And try to dry that hair some more with a towel if you don't want to answer more questions than even you can ask."

eight

Marco was in a joyful mood as he sat before Caravaggio, posing for the nearly life-size portrait of St. John. He was feeling encouraged that Stefano had agreed to find names of some men in high places to help him recover his property. Tomorrow they would meet again. As usual, the artist arranged Marco's body and mantle to match what he had already begun on canvas.

"The chilling rains at last have let up a bit," Marco said in an effort to steer the conversation to light subjects. "It is really too early for the rainy season. Maybe this good weather will hold through the Fall Festival a fortnight hence."

"Could be. The whole city will be there for the festivities, rain or sun. But there is so much mud everywhere. I had in mind some exercise at tennis with my friend Tomassoni. I need to move around after the stress of painting, but I think we have been foiled again. Speaking of foils," he chuckled, "perhaps we will just do some fencing." Caravaggio was hanging the lighted lantern. "Now, Marco, if you will just turn ever so slightly to the right. Head down a bit. Perfect."

Silence prevailed as Caravaggio plunged into his work. Marco's mind wandered to the upcoming meeting with Stefano. He tried to envision their conversation and to consider the next step. But there was too much of the unknown for him to plan ahead. So he let his thoughts fall pleasantly on the subject of Bianca. She was such a complex individual. In his imagination she was serving refreshments. Then he envisioned himself taking her hand and saying to her, "*Signorina,* you are, indeed, lovely. Shall we dance?"

Suddenly Caravaggio let out with a string of oaths and began pacing furiously across the room. When he picked up a ceramic bowl and crashed it on the floor, Marco recoiled. "Are you demon-possessed, man? Surely no flaw on a canvas can generate such an outburst."

"It's not *my* canvas that is flawed. All the so-called artists—Rubens, Borgianni, Tanzio, Orazio Gentileschi, the whole raft of them—they are the demons who are stealing my art! They even call themselves the *Caravaggisti.* They copy my paintings, changing a bit here and there, and claim glory for themselves," the artist shouted. "I let Orazio know about it last night at a tavern. I'd even been to his studio several times and helped him out. This is how he repays me for my suggestions. He steals everything!"

Marco noticed for the first time that Caravaggio's arm was bandaged. "Were you perchance in a fight with Orazio last night?" Marco ventured.

"A harmless scuffle," said Caravaggio, suddenly subdued. "I slashed him—lightly, you understand—across the jaw. That should teach him." He sat down again on the stool behind the easel and began painting as though nothing had happened.

Marco let the *signorina's* lovely hand drift away and concentrated on the strange man on the other side of the easel. It was hard to reconcile the obviously sincere and spiritual man with this violent, irrational one.

"Marco, Marco, you are not the St. John I need," the artist moaned. "You are entirely too cheerful. My St. John is weighted down by the sorrows of mankind. He is grieving over those who are empty inside with nowhere to turn. He is the forerunner of the Lamb of God, who will come to take away their anguish. Show me some anguish, Marco."

Marco frowned and twisted his face grotesquely.

"No, no, stop!" Caravaggio burst out in roars of laughter. "Tell you what; I'll just paint your feet today." He came over and arranged Marco's legs and feet, projecting the left knee toward the canvas with the foot tucked behind into the shadows. The light fell starkly on the bent knee. The artist then painted contentedly for some time. "Ah-ha. Ottavio Costa will be ecstatic over the knees and feet for his altarpiece," he mumbled to himself. Marco restrained a chuckle.

The monotonous swish of the brush continued until a loud knock startled both men. Not waiting for an answer, Ranuccio Tomassoni swung wide the door and entered with a flourish. He set down a bag that appeared to contain rackets and balls. "My good man, the sun is still out. If we are to get a few good matches in before dark, we must be on our way."

"What about the mud?" said Caravaggio, continuing to paint and not even bothering to look up at his friend.

"My cousin has a stone court, well-drained. It is some distance, but if we ride swiftly, we shall still have time. And there is a cozy, little tavern nearby."

"In that case, let us be off." Caravaggio made a quick introduction of the two men to each other. He hurriedly readied himself for more vigorous exercise, while Marco changed back into his street clothes. At the palace exit, Caravaggio turned to Marco and said, "Don't come tomorrow. It's Sunday. I must go atone for my sins. But return the next day—and may you have grief and misfortune in the meantime. It's too late to find another St. John."

❧

On Sunday, threatening clouds again hid the sun. Indeed, it had rained heavily the night before, leaving the cobbled streets slick with mud. Marco chose to ride his fine horse, which would have better footing than he would have. Albret met him at the Marinelli gate, turned his chestnut-colored steed over to a stable hand, and escorted him into the large room where he had previously been received.

When he found himself waiting much longer than before, his high hopes began to diminish under a cloud of apprehension. He was not at all relieved by the serious expression on Stefano's face when he finally entered.

"Good afternoon, Marco," Stefano said in a grave but

fatherly tone. "I have given your request much serious thought. I have even taken some risk upon myself by speaking in general terms with an associate—but all to no avail. I am truly sorry."

Before Marco could respond, Sylvia entered with a tray, pitcher, and two goblets. *Where is the lovely Bianca?* wondered Marco. *I hope she did not fall ill from being caught in the rain. But perhaps it is best that she not see me with these dashed hopes.*

"Signor Marinelli, I am most grateful to you for your efforts," said Marco, trying to conceal his great disappointment. He had failed to prepare himself for such a complete dead end. He prayed silently that God would give him some word that would keep this pathway open.

Immediately a word came to him, the name of the person who had commissioned the St. John painting. "Ottavio," he said, "do you know of an Ottavio Costa? I believe he is in the employ of the state. . . ?"

"He is the official banker. Yes, of course I know of him. Indeed, I have briefly spoken with him on business matters. But, Marco, I could not possibly approach him, even if you were a son of mine. One must always keep one's beliefs private, even in such matters as this."

"Do you have any idea of how he stands on the title-deed issue?"

"No, I do not. Now, if you will excuse me, I have some other matters to attend to." He rang a tiny bell, and Albret suddenly appeared. "Albret, please bring the marchese's horse to the front gate."

❧

As Marco rode slowly through the streets, he tried to sort out his situation and form some kind of plan. He had hung all his hopes on the slim possibility that Signor Marinelli would be able to help. But actually, he had not given a moment's thought to what he would do if that help was not forthcoming.

He had never allowed himself to even consider the possibility of permanently being among the deposed nobles, begging in the streets of Rome.

Even if he could always find employment as a stonecutter, the family would, no doubt, have to give up their one servant. And what about 'Bella? She had her heart set on a good marriage. Without the family's fortune, he would never be able to provide an acceptable dowry—even for a girl from the lower middle-class.

A fine mist filled the air. Marco put on his gloves, pulled his cloak more closely about him, and urged his horse into a trot. Suddenly his mount reared and stepped to the side. A young girl stood in the middle of the street. The gray darkness of the threatening storm had made it difficult to see.

"Please, sir. . . ," the girl said with outstretched hands.

Marco brought his steed to a dancing halt. Before him stood a thin, barefoot girl not much younger than Anabella. There were always beggars in the streets of Rome. At first it bothered him greatly. His mother and sister often went with people from the fellowship of Chiesa Nuova to distribute loaves of bread to them. Marco hardly looked at them anymore. But the round, pleading eyes of this girl arrested him.

"My child, you should not stand in the middle of the street; my horse could have trampled you."

"I'm sorry, but this is the only way I can get anyone to stop. And now you are stopped, see? Will you help me?"

Marco dismounted and knelt before her. "What is your name, and where do you live?"

"That way." The girl pointed in the way he was going. "I've not eaten all day. Neither has my grandmother, who is very sick and is going to die. Please, sir, if you could just give me something for her last meal."

"And your name?" Marco was trying to think fast. A line of Scripture ran through his mind. *"Silver and gold have I none, but such as I have give I thee."* What did he have? A few gold *scudi* in his pouch. Right now it was food she needed, not gold. But there were no shops open or vendors on the streets because it was Sunday.

"My name is Elena, sir."

"My name is Marco," he said simply. He took off his cloak and wrapped it around her. "Would you like to come to my home for a bite to eat? Then we will take some food to your grandmother."

"Yes, I would like that," the girl said solemnly.

Marco placed her on the horse in front of him and rode as quickly as he dared to their humble townhouse.

"I thought you would live in a palace," Elena said when they arrived.

Anabella, always ready to help the unfortunate, was thrilled with a girl visitor of nearly her age. She whisked Elena off to the bedroom to deck her out in warm, dry clothing—complete with shoes.

"Now what is this all about?" said Costanza as she stirred the duck and vegetable soup at the hearth. The servant set another place at the crowded table.

"I don't know," said Marco, shaking his head. "God just dropped her in my lap and said to do for her what I could." He then fleshed out the story in more detail.

"Perhaps, Marco, it would be best if *I* took her to her grandmother's. I have sat with the dying before. I know what to do," said Costanza. "I've been working with the poor, you know, with believers from the fellowship."

"Mother, I am ashamed that I have not. I've come to ignore them in the streets. But I can't let you go out in this weather."

After Elena had eaten heartily, Costanza prevailed, and it was finally agreed that Marco and Anabella would accompany them to Elena's home. Fortunately, the mist had ceased, and the clouds had cleared enough to give a bit more light. It was not a long walk, and Anabella chattered constantly, hardly giving poor Elena time to respond to her many questions. Marco carried a lantern, as the night was bound to fall before they would be safely home again.

To retrace their steps, Marco mentally took note of the many twists and turns in the street, which eventually became a muddy alleyway. Elena stopped in front of a door, next to some stables. "Here," she said, pointing but not offering to open it. "It's not locked."

"I think she's frightened that her grandmother may be worse. She hasn't seen her all day," said Costanza to Marco. "I'll go in first." The others stood outside in silence.

In a few minutes, Costanza emerged. By the light of the lantern, Marco could see that the floor was covered with straw. The room was nearly bare, except for the pallet occupied by the old woman, who was softly moaning.

"Come in, Elena," Costanza said soothingly. "Do you have candles?"

"No."

"That's all right. I brought some." She took the pot of warm soup and bread from Anabella and the blanket roll from Marco. "I'll stay the night. Elena and I will be back for breakfast before you go to work, Marco."

Anabella peeked inside. She was on the point of begging to stay, but the stench changed her mind.

On the way back, Anabella was more subdued. Brother and sister talked about poor Elena, about poverty and illness in general, and about evil and the fear of being harmed. Anabella showed so much understanding and compassion that Marco let the tears run down his face in the dark. He would never forget the big, round eyes in the thin, little face staring up at him in the middle of the street. Elena represented to him the great need of this world.

Back in their clean and warm home, Marco and Anabella knelt in front of the hearth. They prayed that the care and love of Jesus would surround their mother, the grandmother, and little Elena and keep them safe through the night.

nine

On the day of the Fall Festival, the clouds parted, and the sun came out—vigorously going about its job of drying the puddles. Next to Carnival, the celebration of God's blessings on the harvest was the most spectacular event in Rome.

The Marinellis dressed up in their best finery, Bianca in a gown of rich burgundy. Both mother and daughter discreetly wore black eye masks and carried feathered fans, as was the custom for women of their status when appearing at large public gatherings. Although the nominal disguise afforded little protection from those who might wish them harm, ladies enjoyed this mark of distinction and mystery.

All were scarved, hooded, and caped against the morning chill. Albret brought the carriage to the front gate, where the three Marinellis and Sylvia, Albret's mother, climbed in. The center of the festivities, along the Via del Corso, was not far, but, as they would be out most of the day, the vehicle afforded a base and some protection.

❧

Meanwhile, the Biliverti family donned their seldom-worn noble attire. Costanza and Anabella, like the Marinelli women, wore masks. They missed Elena, who until only a few days ago had been sharing their small abode. She had been a total delight, especially for Anabella, who loved and cared for her as if she were a younger sister.

As expected, the grandmother had died during the night with Costanza. Marco enlisted the aid of the fellowship for a small service and burial. Elena cried profusely throughout, but afterward appeared relieved to no longer have to beg and be in constant worry over her only relative. A young couple

61

from the church, who had recently lost one of their three daughters to illness, begged to take her in. With reluctance and sadness, the Bilivertis agreed that it would be best for Elena to have two parents.

The experience with the orphan had a profound effect on Marco. Not only had she opened his eyes to the vast poverty he had ignored, but her presence had unleashed other bravely hidden emotions. He was plagued by worry that his own family might very well be plunged into real poverty if he were unable to find help soon. By trying to stay strong for his mother and sister, he had not taken time to grieve the death of his beloved father. Once emotion had been released, his mind dwelt on this sorrow as well. Needless to say, he was not in a festive mood on this festival day.

᠅

With difficulty the Marinellis found a spot to park the carriage and tether the two horses. Festivities were already in full swing. Musicians wandered among the crowds playing the pipe and tabor; colorfully clad jesters and masked harlequins stirred up roars of laughter as they snaked through their appreciative audience; and delicious aromas of roasting boar and goose wafted from vendors preparing for noon's hunger.

All classes of society mixed freely on such occasions— cardinal and carpenter, noble and servant, artist and patron. All came to enjoy the merriment.

The Marinelli family found themselves drawn to a juggler who was keeping five apples cascading high in the air. He concluded his act by tossing them randomly to the crowd. Bianca reached for an apple and briefly fought a smaller hand for it. Holding the fruit aloft, she glanced toward her competitor.

"Artemisia, how pleasant to see you again," Bianca exclaimed. "Here, I make you a gift of this apple."

Stefano remembered the girl's father, Orazio Gentileschi,

from the lecture he had given on the St. Matthew paintings in the absence of their creator. He promptly introduced himself, Françoise, and Bianca. Orazio in turn presented his wife. The two families strolled together for some time, enjoying the entertainment.

The girls lagged behind, giggling at the wild antics that surrounded them.

"I didn't recognize you in that silly mask, Bianca," said Artemisia. "You are bound to catch the attention of lots of gentlemen with that coy fan of feathers."

"Here, you try it," offered Bianca, with a snicker. She placed the mask on Artemisia and let her flutter her eyes over the fan.

"Ah, Michele Merisi da Caravaggio, could you possibly have been speaking to me?" she chirped in mock sophistication. "You say I am a ravishing beauty? Why, thank you, *signore*."

"I'm sure that's exactly what he would say if he were to see you now," chuckled Bianca. "Now return my props before Mother catches me so exposed."

Artemisia pulled off the mask. "Caravaggio really is here today. We saw him with one of his admirers, Ottavio Costa."

"What did he say, Artemisia?"

"Oh, he didn't see us. My father turned us away. It seems the two of them got in a fight the other night at a tavern."

"Just with words, no doubt."

Artemisia thought it best not to point out the healing slash across her father's jaw. She didn't want to take sides between the two artists, choosing rather to continue to think highly of them both.

Other friends caught the attention of the Gentileschis, and they moved on. The Marinelli family also crossed paths with various acquaintances. Just as they were loading their arms with trays of roasted goose legs, fruit, bread, and marzipan, they heard a young voice whisper somewhat loudly, "That's Bianca Marinelli, the lady artist!"

They turned to meet the blushing face of Costanza Biliverti, who apologized profusely for her daughter's impoliteness. Bianca introduced her parents and assured the Bilivertis that she was flattered to be called "the lady artist."

"Could you perhaps be related to the Marchese Marco Biliverti?" inquired Stefano.

"Indeed, we are, mother and sister."

"How delighted we are to make the acquaintance of his family. Would you care to join us for our little picnic lunch—as our guests?" Stefano offered warmly. With the invitation accepted, Stefano doubled the food on the trays.

The group found a sunny and grassy spot near the carriage, where Françoise spread out two blankets they had brought along. Sylvia and Albret, who had been taking turns watching the carriage, joined them, as did the Biliverti servant. The three sat discretely behind their employers.

As they all were unaccustomed to dining thus, the meal turned out to be a comedy of sorts as they tried without success to balance their food and arrange themselves in a convenient pattern. Costanza and Anabella, who both had a natural penchant for continuous talk, were only slightly constrained by their noble upbringing. Stefano was glad to let them carry the lead in the conversation, while he punctuated it with "How very interesting," and "Please tell us more." Françoise sat ill at ease at the unconventional dining situation, scarcely touching her food.

Bianca was totally fascinated by Marco's mother, so open and willing to talk about every topic—from a serenading lute player to memories of her late husband—a complete contrast to her own mother.

And my friend, the stonecutter, really is a marchese; *though, no doubt, a deposed one,* she thought. *He should be here with us for this strange little meal.* Conflicting emotions welled up in her. She firmly believed her love belonged to Caravaggio—at least to the man she imagined him to be. Yet at the thought of Marco, a calm—warm and comforting—came over her. Both men were here at the festival. Hopefully at least one of them would cross her path.

As if reading her mind, Stefano suddenly said, "And where is the young marchese this day?"

"He has been quite melancholy of late. I believe he prefers to wander around alone," Costanza said forthrightly.

Stefano understood the cause behind the young man's melancholy and wished he had been able to help the family more.

Costanza continued, almost as though she were thinking aloud, "My son is such a compassionate man. Recently he brought an orphan girl to our home. . .the girl stopped him on the street in an attempt to find help for her dying grandmother, the only relative she had."

"I do miss her so," chimed in Anabella. "It was like having a sister. But she needed two parents, so we found some for her."

"How good your whole family is," said Bianca in admiration. She recalled Marco's prayer in the Santa Suzanna. *He is able to do such kind acts, I believe, because he really knows God. I'm not sure that I could rescue an orphan.*

The servants gathered up the scraps and rolled up the blankets.

Costanza said, "We must now go search out my brother and his family. They were to meet us at a certain monument. We lived with them for a while after coming to Rome. He is such a good man. Thank you so much for the generous lunch and good company."

"It was our pleasure to share it with you," Françoise said, with a wan smile. "I do hope we meet again."

At the moment of their departing, an associate of Stefano greeted them. Françoise immediately became more animated. "Giacomo, how delighted we are to come across you by chance. How is your family in Florence?" she said with the utmost interest.

"Very well, thank you, *signora*," he said, kissing her hand.

"Giacomo, this is our only daughter, Bianca Maria," said Stefano. And to his daughter, "This is Giacomo Villani, an associate. He is becoming quite a rising star in the main Medici Bank in Florence. He is in Rome instructing us in some of the new bookkeeping methods they are using there."

The young man of somewhat stout build doffed his velvet cap and bent to lightly kiss her hand. His forked beard was rather damp as it brushed against her fingers. She withdrew her hand quickly and said, "I am always delighted to meet one of Papa's associates. Will you be in Rome long?"

"As long as it takes," he said with a wink at Stefano.

❧

Farther up the Via del Corso, the grand parade was forming. Marco found a place for himself along the street at the front of the crowd. Soon a bevy of trumpeters announced the coming of dignitaries from both church and state. The first group were attired in red velvet trimmed in gold, riding adorned mules. Then came several gilded carriages, followed by nobles and bishops on horseback.

Suddenly Marco gasped at whom he saw riding next to Bishop Mariano—it was none other than his half brother, Jacopo! Their eyes met and a condescending sneer passed across Jacopo's face.

Marco felt anger surge through his body. At that moment he believed all was lost. He had failed his mother and sister completely and had condemned them to a life they were not well suited for. As he made his way back through the crowd, he bumped into a man with a child perched on his shoulder.

"Marco, isn't the parade splendid?" a small voice called out. The man lifted the girl to the ground.

"Elena, my dear little Elena," whispered Marco, his anger melting like snow by a warm fire. "How are you, my beautiful child?"

"She is progressing very well," said the adoptive father,

offering a handshake. "Her new sisters adore her and include her in all their games. They are with their mother, nearer the street. I can never thank God enough—and your family, too—for rescuing her from a miserable existence."

"God does work miracles," said Marco. "Sometimes we forget to trust Him." After a brief visit, Marco moved on. It pleased him to see her so contented with her new family.

ja

Again Elena had given something to Marco—this time, encouragement. *Jacopo is the one triumphant at this moment*, he thought as he strolled through the noisy crowds, *but I will trust in God for victory in the end.* Cockfights, jousting matches, and a donkey race formed the bulk of the next round of entertainment. Uninterested, Marco decided to find his mother and sister. Perhaps they were ready to leave. Instead, he found himself face to face with Caravaggio and Ottavio Costa. The artist introduced his patron to Marco.

"So this is the model for my St. John the Baptist?" said Ottavio, showing surprise. "I thought you were using—shall we say—more ordinary people for models."

"True," said the artist, "but whereas Marco was born to the nobility, he comes to model for me straight from common labor. You are still shaping stones for Maderno at the Santa Suzanna, are you not?"

"Unfortunately, that work is now complete," said Marco. "And I presume the St. John also is nearly finished."

"Then you will return to your castle?" assumed Ottavio.

Lord God in heaven, Ottavio is the name you called to my mind once before. Here he is in the flesh. Please give me the right words to say, Marco prayed. "I do indeed have a castle in Terni, but it is in contest by my brother."

"Ah, your younger sibling is fighting for his half of the land? Stand your ground, my man, stand your ground. If he continues this foolishness, cut him completely out of the inheritance," said Ottavio with conviction.

"He has a bishop pleading his cause. . . ."

"Bishop Ferrante, no doubt. Against his influence, you are bound to lose. He has stolen many lands from their rightful owners and handed them over to those he feels more deserving. Could it be the Bishop Ferrante on his side?"

"I don't know," said Marco evasively.

"Isn't his palace on the Via del Verano, near the university?" broke in Caravaggio. "He bought one of my early paintings of fruit and flowers."

"He's a traitor to tradition all the same," said Ottavio, slapping Caravaggio on the back.

❧

Marco bid them adieu and moved on, looking for his family. He now had a small spark of hope. *Bishop Ferrante, palace near the university, Via del Verano. At last I have an influential name who might favor my cause as the younger brother. And to think, Ottavio assumed I was the elder. Thank you, Lord, for hope.*

He found Costanza and Anabella with the servant in short time. They were watching the Morris dancers, in their colorful costumes, twist and turn to the rhythm of the music. Anabella, especially, was intrigued by the swirling streamers of many colors attached to their shoulders and the tinkling bells on bands around their wrists, knees, and ankles.

They had heard that a couple of farces were to be presented next at the Piazza del Popolo, and they wished to see them before going home. Marco agreed to accompany them.

Though somewhat naughty in parts, the plays were hilarious and left their sides aching from laughter. The merriment was to continue well into the night with dancing, which would begin shortly, but they were all ready to head for home. As they were leaving, they again encountered the Marinellis.

After exchanging a few pleasantries, Costanza remarked, "The dancing will no doubt be the best part of the entire festival—especially for the young ladies and gentlemen. We need to leave, but Marco, you should stay. It will cheer you up for sure."

"That is an excellent idea, Mother. That is, if the lovely Bianca will agree to dance with me. Signor Marinelli, I would be most happy to escort your daughter home afterward. There are torches along the street tonight, and it is only a very short distance from here to the Via Margutta."

Stefano seemed startled by the idea. It took him a few moments to mull over the situation.

"Papa, please, I so seldom have an opportunity to dance. We will not be long," coaxed Bianca, peering over her feathered fan.

Finally Stefano said, "Marchesa Costanza, if you do not have a carriage with you, it would please me greatly to provide your family with a ride home. The thieves will be thick tonight. Marco, I see you have your dress sword at your side. I trust you know how to use it if necessary."

"Indeed, I do. And I am most grateful to you for providing transportation for my family." Marco felt ashamed that he had let his heart deter him from his responsibilities to his family. He admired Stefano for his offer. So it was decided, and Bianca and Marco were left totally alone for the evening.

They found an empty bench where they could await the beginning of the dance. "I've not seen you since the day you rescued me from thugs at the Santa Suzanna," said Bianca, facing him fully, her heart beating wildly within her breast.

"Nor I, you. I was worried that you had become ill from being caught in the heavy rain afterward. You neglected to serve refreshments when I called on your father. . . ."

"Yes, I did suffer congestion and was confined to my bed for a few days. But, you see, I recovered." Bianca removed her mask to prove her good health.

Marco drank in the glowing face and the eyes that sparkled up at him. "You are a beautiful woman, Bianca," he said. "I want to explain why I have been calling on your father."

"You really are a *marchese*. I've figured that out. I'm always left to wonder about situations. My parents are dears to want to protect me so much, but I believe it only brings on more worries. I do have a good imagination." She felt at ease to confess her pent-up thoughts. "Yes, Marco, I would be very pleased to hear what this is all about."

With that encouragement, Marco related in detail how a vast seignory was rightfully his, but, as he had no proof, he was seeking a name of one who would use his influence on his behalf. "Your father was unable to help," he concluded, "but he has been most kind to me—almost with a fatherly tenderness."

"I'm not surprised," said Bianca. After a long pause, she explained, "Mother and I were quite worried that he would actually die of grief when my brother died. He stared into space for days and refused to eat. Since my other brother is away, he probably is allowing you to fill a void."

"Have you asked your father for a painting tutor yet, Bianca?" Marco placed his hands gently around hers.

Bianca felt his warmth and encouragement surge through her. "No, but you have given me courage to do so. I will approach him soon. I also plan to tell him that I do not wish to be betrothed to anyone—that it is my life, and I should have a say in how I live it. I will be able to support myself with my painting—don't you think I could, Marco?"

"Never betrothed?" whispered Marco. Suddenly Bianca became uneasy and withdrew her hands.

For Marco's part, he was in no position to pursue that thought, nor did he wish to jump into the middle of a family disagreement. Thus he chose to divert her thoughts by offering, "Would you like me to arrange a meeting for you with Caravaggio? Perhaps he would allow you to come view the 'St. John the Baptist in the Wilderness' at his studio when it is finished."

"You know I would, Marco! You would do that for me?"

She was stunned by the generosity of his offer. No one had ever before understood her passion to meet this great artist.

"Yes, Bianca, I would do that for you. I hold you in high esteem—and may I have this dance?"

The orchestra, consisting of dulcimers, harps, trumpets, fiddles, and tabors, struck a lively tune. The two were absorbed into the undulating horde of colorfully clad revelers who filled the huge square. They danced the night away, swirling and laughing. Marco refused to let another cut in. Finally, they collapsed on the bench, exhausted.

"I don't know when I've had so much amusement," gasped Bianca, trying to catch her breath.

"Nor I," agreed Marco. "I must get you home as promised." He tilted her chin up toward his face. "You are a remarkable woman," he whispered and kissed her forehead lightly.

As they walked slowly through the torch-lit streets, Marco yearned to hold her closely in his arms. But he knew it was not yet time. Perhaps there would never be a time. They had only tonight for certain. The warmth of the afternoon sun had faded, and a chilling wind began to whip their cloaks. All too soon the dolphin fountain came into view. They arrived at the side entrance, where Sylvia was waiting to open the door for Bianca.

Marco put his hands on Bianca's shoulders and looked down into her upturned face. "I will never forget this evening. Thank you, Bianca, for staying. I will see you again?"

"Yes, Marco."

His hands slid down her arms and clasped her hands. They stood for several moments, searching each other's face. Fire from the street torch reflected in their eyes, burning forever a glow into their memories that would last a lifetime. Slowly Marco let his hands drop from hers, whispered "good night," and disappeared into the darkness.

ten

Bianca awoke late the next morning, stretched, and reminisced about the previous evening with Marco. The magic lingered and engulfed her like the warm coverlet that she pulled up around her. Life seemed whole again. *What difference does it make if Marco ever regains his status as* marchese *or not,* she thought. *He is a wonderful friend and exciting to be with—and he has offered to take me to Caravaggio's studio!*

With Marco's encouragement, she had determined to approach her father today and present him with the plan she had chosen for her life. She rolled over and smiled into her pillow. In the glow of last night, everything seemed possible.

A familiar tap on the door brought her to a sitting position. "Come in, Sylvia," she called.

The servant entered with a tray containing freshly baked bread with jam, goat cheese, and a bowl of warm milk.

"What is this all about?" Bianca questioned. "Since when am I served breakfast in bed—and at this late hour?"

"Your mother ordered it," Sylvia said, half singing the words.

"That makes it more mysterious than ever," Bianca laughed. She washed her face in a cold basin, then crawled back into bed to savor the warm breakfast.

"I know no more than you," said Sylvia with an enigmatic grin, "but something has put your mother in a light-hearted mood this morning.

"Didn't you hear her playing the harpsichord in the little chapel earlier?"

"No, but it always pleases me when Mother is happy."

With Sylvia's help, Bianca was soon dressed for a late church service. Both parents were waiting for her downstairs.

Stefano suggested that they all say prayers in the little family chapel before walking to the church of San Luigi dei Francesi. Bianca was surprised to find candles already burning at the altar. They had not used the chapel since the funeral of the eldest son.

On the way to church, both parents seemed to pay even more attention to their daughter than usual. Finally Stefano said, "Bianca Maria, your mother and I have a matter to discuss with you later this afternoon."

"I trust you will be very happy. . . ," Françoise said, giving her hand a squeeze and smiling at her daughter as they climbed the church steps. Though curious, Bianca was little concerned about the upcoming discussion. After all, her mother hoped it would bring her happiness.

&

After the service, lunch, and siesta, Bianca descended the stairs to the sitting room, as requested. She was delighted to meet with her parents, especially when both seemed to be in a receptive mood. When they finished with their little "surprise," she would take the opportunity to present her plan. Never had she felt more confident.

Both smiling parents soon joined her, followed by Sylvia, with a serving tray of refreshing drinks. When Sylvia made her exit, Stefano turned to Bianca. "My dear daughter, you know your mother and I love you more than life itself. You have brought only joy into our lives."

"And we hope the life we have provided for you has also brought *you* joy," added Françoise.

"Yes," said Bianca, unaware of where this was leading. "You know I love you both, and no matter what my future holds, I will always bless you for the wonderful upbringing you have provided me."

"Do you recall meeting Giacomo Villani at the festival yesterday?" began Stefano.

"No, I don't believe so. You introduced me to many people

we came across. We saw the Bilivertis, the Gentileschis—and an associate of yours, Papa, but I don't recall a Villani."

"Giacomo Villani is the associate you met."

"With the fork-beard?" Bianca recoiled, recalling the repulsion she had felt when he kissed her hand.

"We are delighted to inform you, Bianca Maria, that we have arranged your betrothal to Giacomo Vi—"

"No! Never!" Bianca stood in front of her parents, her eyes flashing. "No, I will never be betrothed—I do not wish to marry. It is my life. You have no right to choose my life for me. What kind of love is that? What could have ever caused you to think I would. . .how could you. . . This is horrid! Have you ever given even one minute to thinking of what I want? Have you?"

"Yes, Bianca, we have," said a startled Françoise. "We only want the best. . ."

"The best? The best, you say," sputtered Bianca, her rage taking over. "What is best for me is to let me learn to paint. You have both told me my work was very good. Were you lying to me? Tell me. You have been plotting this sinister betrothal. . .betrayal it is, rather!"

"Bianca Maria, my dear," said a distraught Stefano. "Yes, your drawings are quite good, remarkable even—for a girl. But, as you know, women cannot possibly possess the creative genius that it requires to become a great artist."

"You must accept this fact, Bianca," said Françoise, her eyes glassy at seeing her daughter thus. "It is the only way."

"I will not accept this so-called fact! Nor will I accept this horrid betrothal! You can disown me as your daughter. . . I'll beg on the streets until I can sell my paintings. I'll. . ."

"Bianca Maria, Giacomo is a fine gentleman with a good mind. He is highly esteemed at the bank," said Stefano to no avail.

Bianca stood over her seated parents, breathing hard, her eyes on fire.

"He will be here with his parents for the be—, for the dinner, in three days. You will be here," said Françoise in a stern voice.

Without another word, Bianca marched out of the room and up the staircase. She could hear her mother's steps heading toward the kitchen. Halfway up the stairs, she realized she had dropped her handkerchief, which she needed for the tears stinging her eyes. Stealthily she crept back to the sitting room. From the hallway she could see that her father's chair was empty, and the desired handkerchief was on the floor—easy to retrieve.

Entering the room, she heard strange, unfamiliar sounds. She paused a few seconds to listen. Uncontrollable sobs were coming from the chapel. She approached and peeked through the crack between the double doors. Papa was on his knees before the altar, head in his hands, trembling and crying out to God.

Instantly Bianca felt remorse for her words crushing out all the anger she had just spewed. How could she have spoken such cruel, selfish words to the papa she so dearly loved? But if she were to open the door to beg his forgiveness, he would be humiliated to be thus exposed.

Slowly, Bianca made her way up to her room. Tears of contrition instead of anger soaked the little handkerchief. She knelt down before the hated *cassone*, making it into an altar.

Father God, she began with the words Marco had used, *I don't know how to pray from the heart with my own words, but I hope you can understand that I am begging for forgiveness for the way I so cruelly spoke to my parents. I certainly was not honoring them as you have commanded—nor was I obeying them. I was so sure that only I knew what was best for my life. I know what I want—my selfish little plan. But I don't want to hurt my parents. I've never seen my papa cry, not even when my brother died, and now I have hurt him*

worse than death. Please, God, forgive me. I will do what
they ask and trust your goodness to work the best for all of
us. In the name of our Lord Jesus Christ. Amen.

Bianca rose from her knees, feeling very much like a
reluctant nun who has given up her life to serve God. Even
though the decision was unselfish and right, the chill in her
bones warned her that the road ahead would not be an easy
one. The range of emotions she had experienced in the past
thirty minutes was more than her body could handle. She
sank limply into her chair with a heavy sigh. What kind of
future did she face now?

༒

Bianca remained in her room through dinner, too exhausted
to weep. After passing a restless night, she finally fell into a
deep sleep at dawn, thus missing the morning meal. No tap at
the door from Sylvia. Bianca spent the morning with needlework, pricking her fingers and sighing. By noon, delicious
odors from the kitchen reminded her that life must go on.
Her hands trembled from weakness, causing mistake after
mistake. Hunger pains stabbed at her stomach. Yet she was
too ashamed to face her parents.

Finally, when she was sure lunch had passed, she crept
down to the kitchen. Sylvia was clearing the table.

"Well, good afternoon," said Sylvia, unwinding the cloth
she had just wrapped around the bread. "I figured hunger
would eventually bring you out. I'll fix you a plate from
what's left."

"Oh, Sylvia, I feel so terrible. My life is over before it's
begun," sighed Bianca.

"I know. . .I know all about your 'terrible' life," said
Sylvia, setting a steaming plate on the table. "I heard your
parents talking at lunch. . . ."

"Please don't mock me, Sylvia. I feel bad enough."

"My dear, you probably don't feel any worse than your
papa. Or your mother, either, for that matter. Poor lady; she

never lets on about how she feels."

"That's true, Sylvia. I've been so remorseful over how I spoke to Papa and haven't even thought how poor Mother must feel. She was so happy about the 'wonderful' news they were going to share with me."

"Maybe this Giacomo fellow will turn out better than you imagine. Have you thought. . ."

"Sylvia, don't try to convince me. I've already decided that I will sacrifice my life to their wishes. Of the two pains in my heart, hurting them is the most severe. But I'm repulsed by the man they have chosen—perhaps I would feel this way about anyone to whom I must be betrothed, I don't know. However, I recall disliking him when they introduced us at the festival—before I knew. . . . It was a planned introduction, I now know. They pretended it was a chance meeting. Sylvia, what am I to do?"

"Well, your papa is still in the courtyard. He's not left yet for the bank. . . ."

"I'll go talk to him. I can't bear this estrangement," said Bianca, rising.

೩

Stefano stood when he saw his daughter. They faced each other for a few moments in silence. Both were well aware of a father's legal right to disown—even imprison—a recalcitrant child. Bianca saw a care-worn face, more aged than she remembered. Her father clearly was unaware of the agony she had witnessed through the crack in the chapel door. He was the first to open his arms. Bianca eagerly fell into the offered embrace.

"My precious, sweet Bianca Maria. You are the joy of my life and always will be."

"Papa. . .please, I don't deserve. . ." They both sat on the long stone bench she had often shared with him since childhood.

"Bianca Maria, the betrothal stands. The dinner stands," he

said directly. Then he continued in a softer tone, "But there is much we can talk about. Tell me all that is in your heart, and I will listen."

"Papa, you are so good, and I am so undeserving. I didn't mean the terrible words I said yesterday. I know you and Mother love me very much and want to arrange for me the best life possible. I am truly sorry. Please forgive me."

"You are forgiven, my dear. Now continue."

Bianca sobbed into her little handkerchief, then somehow found the strength to tell him, "I know it is unheard of, but I so wanted to be a professional artist—to learn how to paint with oils. Maybe I would have failed completely, but I was prepared to ask you if you could find a tutor for me. That made the betrothal seem a double blow." Bianca paused, then, calmly and with little emotion, said, "But I will submit to your wishes."

"Thank you. Now, let me present the reality of the situation." Stefano had his usual businesslike voice back. "Of course you could remain with us in this villa for a few more years. . .but, although you are a very beautiful and desirable young woman, with each year the list of fine unmarried gentlemen diminishes. Your dowry is adequate. . .I've been saving and investing for it since your birth. . .but it is not abundant. A man wants a *young* woman who will bear him children."

Bianca sat quietly, hardly hearing this message of harsh reality.

"Giacomo Villani comes from a fine family. Your mother and I met his parents while they were vacationing in Rome a few months ago. They are not wealthy, but are good stock. Giacomo, on the other hand, has risen rapidly in the banking business. He has a quick mind, is innovative in business—a man of integrity. You know I would only choose the best for you. He is in the process of building a villa in Florence for his future family. As you know, Florence is as much—if not more—of an art center as Rome. As time allows, I feel sure he would indulge your interest."

"Indulge?" Bianca felt the heat of anger again creep up her neck. "I don't want to just have my interest indulged from time to time. . . ."

"Please hear me out, Bianca Maria.

"It speaks very well of the man that he wants to have everything in order before the marriage actually takes place. Yet he is eager for this betrothal to be finalized. He was more than pleased with you—as I knew he would be. He has requested that you wait two years to be married, as he wishes to have the villa complete and furnished."

"Two years? I have two years?" Bianca smiled at the pleasant extension of her "life."

"Yes, my dear. At eighteen I believe you will be much more receptive to the idea of marriage. I will make every effort possible to provide opportunities for the two of you to spend some time getting to know each other. We can visit your brother in Florence. I feel I neglected that part of my parental duty before—with Roland."

"Has Reginoldo met—this man?"

"I don't believe so. But—and you will be pleased to know—your brother will be here for the betrothal dinner."

"That will make it bearable."

"And there is something else I want to share with you," Stefano said with a smile and a slight twinkle in his eye.

Bianca had had her fill of surprises, but she remained subdued and listened, as was her duty.

"I have sent a message by courier this morning," he began, watching Bianca closely for her reaction, "to Orazio Gentileschi, an artist of no less stature than your Caravaggio. He instructs his daughter, Artemisia, in painting. I thought that perhaps he might have a place for another girl to learn in his studio."

"I don't understand, Papa," she said, rather dazed. "You

seem to be directing my life in two opposite directions."

"If he is willing, that would give you two years to devote to your art. Enough time to see what you can do. Does that please you?"

"Yes, yes, of course, Papa," she said, giving him a sincere hug. *I want a whole life devoted to painting,* she thought, *but two years, when it seemed I had nothing, is good.* "That is very thoughtful of you. I am most pleased." But Bianca also remembered how her father had thought it only right for his wife to give up composing music when she married. It would definitely be only two years.

eleven

Two days after the festival, Marco walked toward the Palazzo Madama for his final sitting. The magical evening with Bianca had been pushed aside as an unrealistic dream. Too much had to transpire before he could turn his mind to such personal longings. Thus the thought of her brought more sadness than joy. Even though her feeling for Caravaggio was a passion he coveted for himself, the most he could do for her at this time was to arrange a meeting for her with the artist. That he determined to do.

He thought of little Elena, who had opened his eyes to poverty and misery. When needy situations presented themselves, he now tried to respond in the way Christ would have him to. At that moment he noticed a man huddled beside the street with his hands over his head. He was naked from the waist up. As Marco approached, he heard deep sighs. "Here, man," he said, wrapping his own cloak about the mendicant's shoulders. "When I return, I will bring you some bread and a few gold coins."

"*Grazie, grazie*, God bless ye," mumbled the man without looking up.

❧

By the time Marco arrived at the studio, his heart beat heavily with despair over his own misfortunes and the magnitude of the world's misery.

"Don't bother to change clothes, Marco. It's the face I must capture today." The artist hung his lantern and immediately set to work.

There's a small bakery not far from here. I'll buy the man some bread—maybe get some fruit. Then I'll sit and talk with

81

*him, find out what his troubles are. I'm sure they are worse
than my own. And, as usual, I'll be paid with gold coins. I
can spare a few. I'll share the love of God with him.* Marco
dwelt for some time on the man beside the street. He rated
himself a mediocre Samaritan. A *good* Samaritan would have
stayed and talked right then and there and been late for the
sitting. From there his mind pondered the immensity of problems and his own inability to solve them.

Suddenly Caravaggio exclaimed, "Marco, my good man,
you have finally captured the soul of St. John the Baptist. For
generations to come, people will gaze on this face and understand what the cousin of Jesus understood—our lives are full
of misery and sorrows, but when we come face to face with
the Lord Jesus Christ, and repent, He can lift us above these
earthly woes. Come see for yourself."

Marco was amazed at Caravaggio's creation. He gazed not
only into a mirror of his own downcast eyes, but also into the
reflection of the deeper thoughts of his heart. "You have portrayed exactly my feelings, Caravaggio. The Lord has indeed
bestowed upon you a great gift."

"I only painted the grief and sorrow I saw on your face—
and that expression corresponds precisely with the sorrow I
sought. Come, let's celebrate the successful completion of
this work to God's glory," said the artist, slapping Marco on
the back and thrusting into his palm double the usual wages.

He led his model back through the several large kitchens,
heartily greeting all the workers as they went. It was nearing
the time of the evening meal, and a great deal of baking, roasting, and other forms of preparation were in progress. Caravaggio grabbed a large platter and began slicing a bit of roasted
boar here, a hunk of cheese there; he picked up a round loaf of
freshly baked bread and various other delicacies.

"Pull up a couple of stools here." He indicated a large
wooden table, then disappeared. Marco did as he was bid.
His host reappeared with two goblets filled with drink. "Let

us thank the Lord for this good work He has done through me," he said and began praying rapidly, ending with a jubilant, "Amen, and praises be to the Lord."

"Is the Cardinal del Monte throwing a banquet tonight?" asked Marco as he sampled the food.

"Oh, no, not at all. The cardinal is seldom in residence. The palace, however, must be kept in operating condition at all times. All the servants, the groomsmen, the chaplains, the guards, et cetera, et cetera—they all must be fed. The cardinal is a generous man. I owe a great deal to his patronage. My fame began with the St. Matthews that he commissioned, you know. Some of my paintings hang in this palace, also."

"You mentioned a Bishop Ferrante at the festival—you said he had bought one of your earlier paintings. Is he also a patron?" asked Marco, hoping for more information about the bishop who might be in a position to help him.

"No, not really. He just bought the painting because he liked it. Nice fellow, though."

"I've not met him, but I have a matter to discuss with him, a legal matter of much importance. . . ."

"About that lost castle, no doubt. Well, then, my dear Marco, let me write a letter of introduction." At that he called a young lad over and requested that he bring him paper, ink, and quill. "I won't present you as my model, but as a dear friend and fellow parishioner."

As Caravaggio scribbled along, Marco was aware that he could make almost any request and Caravaggio would gladly grant it today, so gleeful was he over the successful completion of his painting. In fact, Marco did have another request.

"Thank you. I am, indeed, indebted, to you for your kindness," said Marco, folding the letter and placing it inside his doublet.

"Anything for a friend," said Caravaggio. "Anything else?"

"Yes, actually there is something. I am acquainted with a lovely young lady, Bianca Marinelli, who makes most excellent charcoal sketches. She admires your work and has a remarkable understanding of it. It would please both of us if you would be so kind as to invite her to your studio to meet you and to see the amazing 'St. John' that you have just completed."

"A girl artist, huh? Well, it does happen. Women are treated terribly in the art world, however. They're forbidden to draw from live models, can't be favored with more than one apprenticeship, are told that no matter how hard they try, they can never possess the creative genius that belongs to maleness. Silly idea, if you ask me. Sure, bring her over. Signor Costa is having the painting delivered to him on Saturday. Why not come here right after siesta on Friday?"

"She will be so delighted. Thank you."

"Bianca who, did you say?"

"Marinelli."

"I've heard that name recently," said Caravaggio, scratching his head. "Let me think. Ottavio introduced me to a certain Giacomo Villani at the festival. That's it. We spent a good deal of time together enjoying the merriment. I'm sure he said he had just made the acquaintance of the woman to whom he is to be betrothed—Bianca Marinelli, I'm sure it was Marinelli. Would that be the same young lady?"

Marco blanched. How many young Bianca Marinellis could there be in Rome?

❧

Bianca gathered her pages of parchment and charcoal sticks and called Albret to accompany her to the Piazza del Popolo. At the moment of departure, they heard the voice of Françoise ask, "Bianca, Albret, may I accompany you today?" She suddenly appeared, pulling on her cloak and hood. "This is, no doubt, the last fair day we will be granted for some time."

"Yes, Mother, I'm delighted you wish to come with us," said Bianca with surprise.

Mother and daughter walked briskly in the crisp air, chatting of mundane affairs. Albret trailed, lugging the art supplies. They found a bench in the piazza with the sun to their backs. Two dogs were scrapping with a bit of rag, each tugging to win it from the other. Bianca chose them as the subject of her sketch and began to compose the general design.

"Bianca, there are some things I wish to tell you," said Françoise, shifting her position. "You know how your father and I have shielded you from unpleasantness. We have wanted to protect you from the cruelty of this world. Perhaps that has caused you to imagine that you live in an ideal world where all dreams are possible." She paused for a receptive signal from her daughter.

Bianca laid her sketch aside. "Mother, surely Papa has told you that I will submit to your wishes, although it is not the life I would have chosen for myself."

"Yes, of course he has. We keep no secrets from each other," said Françoise. "It is painful to know of your displeasure, even as we are pleased that you are graciously accepting our choice. I was so hopeful that you would be happy—and I believe eventually you will be—though your father expected some difficulty. Neither of us were prepared for that outburst. All is forgiven, however. But you need to understand why we have made this decision for you. You need to understand what our lives have been. . . ."

"Mother, I have always wanted to know. Your past life seems shrouded in mystery."

"Shrouded in *misery*, one might say! You know that I grew up in La Rochelle, France. La Rochelle was a prosperous port, and although our lives were simple, there was virtually no real poverty. Our family lived in the town, but we had a small farm on the outskirts. The church was the center of all our social as well as religious activity.

"My mother read a passage from the Bible every night, and then my father would pray. Afterward he would play the harpsichord that had belonged to his father. He taught me to play, and, when I was accomplished enough, I would accompany the singing of a hymn before going to bed. Ours was a loving and close family. Not only were there six of us children, but we had countless cousins and neighborhood children around. We worked and played together. I knew, even as a small child, that there were civil wars in France, but it had not yet touched us.

"When hundreds of refugees began moving into our town, we started to hear details of the wars. It seemed to be all about politics and power. The government was afraid our party was becoming too large in number and would take over. I couldn't understand why the French were fighting each other. It made no sense.

"La Rochelle has two great towers at the entrance of our port. A huge, heavy chain is pulled across between the two at night to keep out unwelcome ships. The first battle I remember, the chain was pulled to keep out an onslaught of government ships. When they refused to turn back, men of the town threw rocks and poured boiling oil from the towers—then cast down torches to set them on fire. That was the beginning of misery.

"We no longer went to the church but worshiped in each other's homes. With almost constant fighting in the streets, it was no longer safe to go outdoors. My oldest brother was shot and later died from his wound."

"Mother, I am so sorry you had to endure all that," said Bianca, greatly moved by these revelations. But Françoise didn't hear, as she was in another world, another time.

Looking straight ahead, she continued, "Finally, after eight years, the fighting stopped. Then, not long afterward, on the feast day of Saint Bartholomew, the sister of our young King Charles was to marry Henri of Narvarre. Since Henri was of our party and could eventually lay claim to the French throne, those who were for him went wild with celebration. Thousands gathered in Paris for the wedding. A rumor was sent abroad—probably by the Queen Mother, Catherine de

Medici—that their true intent was to assassinate King Charles. As a result, thousands were slain in the streets.

"Many from La Rochelle had gone to Paris; few returned. Then the fury arrived in our town. Our house was torched and our family murdered—my father and three little ones. Only my mother, myself, and my younger brother Etienne were able to escape."

"I thought your family died of the plague," said Bianca, horrified at this tale of woe.

"The rest of my family, yes, did eventually die of an illness. It could have been the plague, I don't know. That was in August 1572. I was sixteen. The three of us wandered south, walking at night, sleeping during the hot summer days. We had taken nothing with us and had no idea where we were going. We prayed constantly for God's protection. By moonlight we took vegetables from family gardens and helped ourselves to milk from a friendly cow or goat. Mother reminded us of how the apostles had eaten grain from the fields when they were hungry.

"One morning we took refuge in a barn attached to a family dwelling. It was well past time to feed the animals, so we felt safe to take rest there on the hay. I awoke with a start out of a sound sleep. Standing over us with his hands on his hips was the owner of the barn. Since we were obviously strangers to the region, I fully expected to be slain on the spot. I shook Mother's arm, and she immediately sat up.

" 'You are, indeed, a ragged bunch,' the man said with a heavy accent. He made the sign of the cross and insisted we come inside his house. His wife was equally kind, but spoke hardly any French. She showed us where we could bathe and brought us all clean clothing. By the time we again looked human, she had filled the table with bountiful dishes. Cooked food never tasted so good. Their two sons came in from the fields and joined us.

"Naturally, we were frightened to tell our story, but they

easily guessed by our simple dress and the fact that we were wandering about, that we had fled from the war in La Rochelle. Mother even told about the murder of her husband and children. As it turned out, the family also had been refugees, from Italy, only a few years back. He told us how others had helped his family get out of Milan during wars there. 'The French peasants helped us get settled, even sold us this land,' I remember him saying."

"Wasn't that family endangered by taking you in?" asked Bianca, thoroughly intrigued, as well as saddened, by her mother's story.

"Yes," said Françoise, looking into her daughter's face and, for the first time since she had begun her story, allowing tears to stream down hers. "Yes, Bianca, we stayed with the family for about a week. Then the man arranged for us to come to Italy, to Milan, where we were sheltered by his brother's family. We learned later that the man was tried and convicted of harboring refugees and put to death. His name was Peter Marinelli."

"Marinelli!" Bianca exclaimed.

"Yes, Bianca. He was your grandfather. Later, his son Stefano returned to Milan, also. He lived at his uncle's house for a brief period while we were there. Long enough for us to become betrothed. Then he was apprenticed to a banker in Florence. Suddenly, little Etienne died. Then a week later, on the same day, Stefano's uncle and his wife died. And finally my mother. . .I don't know if it was the plague. I had been sent to care for two small children in a stranger's home. I wasn't even there when they all died."

"Then you and Papa were married?"

"Yes. I didn't love him then, but I had great respect for him and his family. During the year that I was in his uncle's household, I had begun to compose on the harpsichord and on the lute. It provided a wonderful escape for me. I was obsessed with the idea that I could sell my compositions and make my way in the world."

"Like me and my painting?"

"Yes, Bianca. But that is foolishness. A woman cannot compete with men in this world. We will always lose. Believe me, dear daughter, you will be most happy if you accept the good that comes your way—cherish it—and don't ever attempt to fight against power. You will lose the good you have. There is no better man than your father. Trust him. He is wise and only wants the best for you."

"Yes, Mother, I understand what you are telling me." *But, Mother*, she wanted to scream, *how can you believe that women cannot achieve? Why else would God give us the talent—and the yearning?* The two embraced and let the tears be the words to express the depth of their feelings.

twelve

Marco had left the feast at the Palazzo Madama much later than planned. He deliberately took advantage of Caravaggio's generous mood to ask one more favor: food for the beggar he had met on the way. Unfortunately, the man was no longer where he had encountered him earlier. Marco felt he had learned another lesson in following the Lord's command to care for our neighbors in need: Respond immediately, or the opportunity may pass. In a short time, however, he came across three poor children playing in the street, who were happy to devour the unexpected food.

Once home, Marco wasted no time in penning a letter to Bishop Ferrante, requesting an audience. He sent it by messenger, along with Caravaggio's letter of introduction, and prayed for a positive response. Hadn't Ottavio said Cardinal Ferrante was "a traitor to tradition"?

⁂

The positive response arrived on Wednesday morning. It was delivered on horseback—a page from the bishop's court. Marco responded to the loud knocking at the door and stepped outside.

"I am looking for the Marchese Biliverti. This is the building to which I was directed, but. . ."

"Yes, I am in truth the *marchese*. Please pardon my humble attire. What news do you have, my lad?"

"Have you sent letters recently to a bishop?" inquired the boy, attempting to verify Marco's identity.

"Yes, I have. To the Bishop Ferrante, whose residence is on the Via del Verano."

Appearing satisfied, the page continued, "The Bishop

Ferrante will see you this afternoon at four of the clock. He is leaving on a rather long journey tomorrow and wishes to hear your case before departing. Present this card at the gate." The page then proceeded to instruct Marco in the etiquette of presenting oneself in the audience chamber.

Marco thanked him with a gold coin and requested that the page convey to the bishop his deep appreciation and inform him that he would be there at the appointed time.

2&

At exactly four in the afternoon, Marco presented himself at the gate, dressed appropriately as one of the old nobility. He was escorted up a flight of stairs and down a wide hallway. He was asked to wait outside the large double doors while his presence was being announced.

After perhaps five minutes, he was ushered into a long room with an elevated chair at the other end. The gray-bearded churchman was pulling his robe around himself as though he had just sat down. Several other people were in the room—guards, pages, young priests. Marco noted the huge windows that opened toward sculptured gardens. The walls were adorned with tapestries and a few large paintings in gilt frames.

Marco stood between two guards, one of whom whispered, "You see that large, black tile three-fourths of the way down? The three of us will slowly walk to it, and that is where you will stand." Marco nodded, and they proceeded.

When Marco arrived at his place, the bishop spoke. "You may approach." A priest handed the bishop two letters, which he slowly opened and took his time reading.

"So you are a friend of the famous Michele Merisi da Caravaggio. Do you like the painting I have purchased from him?" The bishop waved his arm toward the painting of an arrangement of various fruit, flanked by freshly picked flowers.

"Yes, *Monsignore*," said Marco, keeping his eyes lowered. "I find he. . ."

"Marchese Marco Biliverti, is it?" interrupted the bishop. "I don't have much time."

"Yes, I am he."

"I have a reputation for defending those with a just cause against the tyranny of tradition—as you are probably aware. However, the cause must have merit. My family comes from Terni, and I knew your father and had great respect for him. The last time I saw him, Jacopo was just a toddler and the joy of his father's existence. I learned only recently, when I was in Terni, that he had married again after Jacopo's mother died.

"And, I am sorry to say, I heard many rumors about you, the much younger second son. They are saying in Terni that you abandoned your studies at the university to steal the land and castle from your brother, attempting to force your ill father to sign a will that would name you sole heir. Having failed that, you convinced him that Jacopo would never return and made him sign a letter of disinheritance that was sent to your brother in Madrid. That letter, of course, would be null and void without a signed and recorded will to that effect.

"When I received your request for an audience, I was curious to meet you. I am willing to hear your side, but I must tell you, you are not well thought of in your hometown."

Marco had been forewarned that Jacopo was spreading malicious and false rumors about him, but he was surprised and angered that they had reached the bishop's ears. With as much composure as he could muster, he said, *"Monsignore*, I am grateful for the opportunity to clear my name. To begin with, my father was not ill when he called me home from my studies, but needed help supervising the harvest. It was at that time that he informed me of changing his will and disinheriting my half brother."

Marco continued to relate the truth of the situation, including Jacopo's refusal to even provide for his stepmother and sister. "Jacopo has enlisted the aid of Bishop Mariano, whom perhaps you know. He was a friend of my father's, but like yourself, had no knowledge of recent events."

"Ah, the Bishop Mariano, always the advocate for the first-born, regardless of circumstances. . . . I am leaving for Perugia tomorrow and will pass through Terni. I have investigators in my employ who are quite skilled in discovering the truth of a situation. When I return, if indeed I have found your case to be a just one, I will send you word. You are dismissed." With that the bishop abruptly left the room and Marco was escorted out by the way he had entered, not knowing whether to be happy or disturbed.

ঌ

On this same Wednesday morning there was much bustling about in the Marinelli household. Reginoldo had arrived by carriage the night before from Florence, accompanied by his personal servant. Bianca was delighted to see her brother after his absence of nearly a year. He seemed older and wiser, perhaps due to the newly grown beard. There had been no opportunity to talk with him alone until this morning.

"*Sorellina*, little sister," Reginoldo said, taking Bianca's hand and drawing her into a small alcove next to the stairway. "Surely you can spare a few minutes from these happy preparations for your adoring brother." They sat in brocaded chairs facing one another.

"Reginoldo, you are the only happiness in this otherwise dreadful day," Bianca confessed. "Mother encouraged me to suggest dishes for the dinner tonight, but my heart is not in it. She thought it would be a nice touch if I prepared something—to impress that man."

"*That* man? Bianca, are you telling me you are not pleased with the choice Papa has made for you?"

"I've agreed to follow their wishes out of love and respect for them—and also because I really have no other choice." Bianca then proceeded to tell of the outburst toward their parents, the reconciliation, and their father's agreement to allow her to study painting for the two years before her marriage.

"That seems more than fair to me, Bianca. Papa always did give in to your wildest whims," consoled Reginoldo with a condescending smile. "I have not met Giacomo, but I have been past the villa he is having built in Florence. It is larger than our own. I understand he is planning fountains, gardens, and walkways. . . ."

"Reginoldo, I don't care about *his* villa!" interrupted Bianca. "It will be a prison to me. And don't talk down to me as though I were a simple, ignorant child."

"Bianca, I'm truly sorry," said Reginoldo, taking her hands and looking into her face. "I didn't mean to take lightly your situation. You certainly are no longer the little sister I used to tease. You are a beautiful, intelligent woman. There is nothing I can do to reverse this betrothal, but I will promise you this: If Giacomo does not treat you as he should, he will have to answer to me. I will keep my eye on him in Florence."

Bianca was forced to laugh at the image of Reginoldo following around after "old Fork-Beard" to see if he were behaving himself. "Just help me get through this ordeal today. Kick my shins if I say something I shouldn't, and kick his shins—if he so much as looks at me," said Bianca, trying to make a joke out of an all-too-serious matter.

"See? I'm wearing my kicking boots," he chuckled.

"Now, brother, tell me what it's like to study law at the university."

Reginoldo lapsed into relating a series of anecdotes, many enhanced by exaggeration, about the antics of professors and his peers. Bianca found him delightfully entertaining.

❧

By late afternoon, every article in the house had been scrubbed and polished, all the special dishes were prepared, and lighted candles and garlands decorated the sitting room, chapel, and dining area. As extra cooks had been hired, Sylvia was free to assist Bianca in her dressing and grooming.

She wore a blue velvet gown with high collar in back and

open throat. Françoise had loaned her a ruby pendant to complete her attire. Sylvia suggested braiding only on the crown, under a dark velvet cap, allowing her hair to cascade loosely at the back. Bianca hardly glanced in the mirror before assuring Sylvia that all was fine.

Giacomo arrived with his parents and an aunt. The parish priest performed the betrothal ceremony in the family chapel. Bianca never looked directly at her fiancé. Somehow she felt that none of this had anything to do with her. She was doing her duty as she had promised to do.

At dinner, succulent courses came and went. Giacomo sat directly across from Bianca. He was flanked by Reginoldo on his left and his parents on his right. Stefano and Françoise sat at the ends of the lengthened table. Bianca picked at her food and finally stole a glance at her betrothed, who was in animated conversation with her father about the efficacy of loaning money to sea merchants.

The reddish beard bobbed up and down with his words. His mustache formed the bristles of two very large paint brushes, coming to points and indicating opposite directions. Then the swallowtail beard—as it was properly called—became two enormous brushes, flaring out beneath the twins above and leaving such a division that a tip of the chin was visible at their parting. His fork, held in pudgy fingers, worked steadily to keep the delicacies moving toward his mouth; yet the food seemed to have totally vanished when he spoke.

His nose was prominent, and his shoulders were somewhat rounded under his burgundy doublet, but he was not an ugly man. His attire, and even the horrid beard, were neat in the extreme.

"My son tells me you already have a *cassone*, filled with a wardrobe. Is that so, Bianca?" Signora Villani said loudly.

"Excuse me, I failed to hear what you said to me," Bianca said with a blush, having forgotten that this whole affair was in her honor.

"The *cassone*—you have one, I understand, my dear? I thought perhaps you would allow me to go through it and see what you are lacking. A young woman always lacks something."

Bianca smiled at her future mother-in-law, assuming she was thinking of a gift she could add. "Any addition would be appreciated," she said.

"I was thinking more of helping you determine what items are missing that you would need in Florence. The styles are different in our fair city, my dear—for example, women of our station wear a high neckline," she stated. "You do have two whole years to complete your wardrobe, though."

Bianca instinctively put her hand to her throat. Her dress was a modest cut, not at all revealing, but suddenly she felt exposed. "I will try to dress appropriately" was all she could manage to say. But she could feel the anger creeping up her neck to her ears, turning them hot.

Françoise graciously saved the moment by inquiring about the pottery made in Florence. The *signora* turned toward her and launched into a discourse of more than anyone would care to know about pottery.

Soon one of the hired cooks arrived, holding aloft a great pie with golden crust, which was by now the fourth course. With a flourish he set it in the center of the table and began reciting the marvelous ingredients: "Pork, goose, sausage, onion, cheese, eggs, almonds, dates, sugar, spices, et cetera, et cetera. Please enjoy it to the fullest." The supposedly happy couple were served first. *Will this never end?* thought Bianca.

The dinner finally did terminate with sweets and the new and popular drink in Rome—coffee. Now it was time for the merriment to begin. Servants pulled the furniture back against the wall in the sitting room to make space for dancing. As all stood, the two fathers shook hands and made short speeches about how two great families would soon be joined.

As all watched, Giacomo took Bianca's hand, bowed low, and said, "I am delighted that you will be my bride. I humbly hope to be worthy of the trust your father has placed in me. And now, Bianca, may I have this dance?"

Bianca stiffened, but nodded agreement. She allowed him to put his arm about her waist and guide her around the room as three hired musicians struck up a recognizable tune. Françoise beamed as Stefano took her in his arms. The older Signor Villani had scarcely spoken during dinner because he hardly needed to; his wife had begun many a conversation with, "My husband and I think. . ." Nevertheless, they joined the dancing. Reginoldo was left to squire the aunt, and the priest chose this moment to depart.

Soon partners were changed, and Reginoldo caught his sister and whispered in her ear, "I thought I was going to have to kick your shins when the Villani woman started stirring around in your *cassone.*"

"Her eyes will never get the tiniest glimpse inside," said Bianca resolutely.

"Perhaps I should have kicked *her* shins," whispered Reginoldo.

It was past midnight when Signora Villani announced that they must soon bid the Marinellis goodnight. They had all arranged to stay at an inn on the way to Florence so that they could get a good start the next day. Stefano suggested the newly betrothed couple might enjoy a few minutes alone in the alcove. Chairs were pulled out from the wall, and the rest of the group settled into conversation.

Giacomo and Bianca dutifully sought the alcove, but as there was no door, they were hardly alone. "I'm so very sorry that I must leave Rome tonight. I promise to return soon. Your father has even mentioned that he would bring you to Florence from time to time. Would you like that, Bianca?"

"Yes, that would be fine."

"For your sake, I also regret that our marriage will not take place for two years. You see, whatever I do, I must do well. The villa must be complete and furnished in every detail. I plan for the gardens to be planted this spring. That will give them a year's growth before we move in."

"I have agreed to the two years. In fact, Papa is finding me a tutor so that I may pursue my art training."

"I am doing well in the banking business," continued Giacomo, totally ignoring her remark. "There will be enough servants to care for the daily maintenance of my villa, but I will expect you to learn to care for my garments. Mother does that now, but she can show you what I am accustomed to. We can talk of my other expectations on my next visit."

With that remark, Giacomo rose and kissed Bianca's hand. He called Albret to have his horses harnessed to his carriage, and Bianca wiped her hand with her handkerchief and ran up the stairs.

thirteen

Thursday morning found the Marinelli family partaking of a late breakfast together. Françoise and Stefano had taken great pleasure in the previous evening's festivities. They were invigorated by the hope that new love would bud and grow, spawned by their careful matchmaking. Their aspiration for the young couple had spilled over into their own hearts, awakening their own passion, which burned far into the night after their guests had departed. Indeed, an outsider would have thought by the blush on the mother's cheeks that she was the newly betrothed.

An awkward silence lingered over the table, each family member guarding private thoughts. Bianca dipped her bread in warm milk and prayed that no one would ask her about Giacomo. In truth, her parents were reticent to ask. Reginoldo dismissed all the comments or questions that came to his mind as not being benign enough, and kept silent.

Suddenly Albret appeared at the door and rescued the moment. "Signor Marinelli, I have just been handed this communication from a messenger at the gate." He handed Stefano a paper, then took his leave.

The father read in silence, without expression, then looked up and smiled. "Bianca Maria, this communication is from Orazio Gentileschi. I think you will be pleased." He then read aloud:

> *Dear Signor Marinelli,*
> *I was surprised, and flattered, to receive your inquiry as to whether I would consider taking your daughter as an apprentice in my studio alongside my own daughter.*

I must say that Artemisia thought it a wonderful idea and presented bountiful reasons why it would be advantageous for all.

I did give the idea serious consideration but have decided that with the number of commissions I am receiving, I simply do not have the time to devote to another student.

However, knowing as I do the difficulty that young women of talent face, I have taken the liberty to inquire of a certain Lavinia Zapponi (whose name you may know, as she has acquired some fame) if she would accept an apprentice. She was tutored by her father, who was a follower of the esteemed Raphael. Unlike most women artists who are known mainly for their portraits, she specializes in narrative works. She and her husband, the artist Paolo Salviati, have recently moved to Rome from Bologna, as she has been appointed an official painter to the state.

In spite of her new official duties, she is interested in instructing Bianca Maria if she can show superior ability and the discipline to work long, tedious hours with diligence. She invites you and your daughter to come to her home for an interview. Have the prospective student bring a minimum of two dozen of her finest sketches. One week from this day at four of the clock would be convenient for her. . . .

An address and manner of contact was included in Orazio's letter.

All the joyful excitement that Bianca had been expected to feel the night before now surged through her body. "Papa, she paints for the state and wants to meet me!" she finally gasped.

"*She* wants to meet you," echoed Reginoldo, pleased for his sister. "A famous woman artist with a girl student. That's unique."

Françoise stiffened, the color draining from her face. "Stefano, why was I not informed that you had written such a letter?" she said in controlled indignation.

In truth, Stefano had not told his wife because he had written the letter to appease Bianca, with little thought that a tutor might actually be found. "Françoise, you were so busy. . .occupied with all the preparations. . . ."

"But Mother, I have two years before my marriage, two glorious years to pursue my heart's desire."

"We cannot deny her this, Françoise. It is her heart's desire," said Stefano a bit sheepishly, echoing his daughter's words. "When that time is up, she will be eager to settle into her new home, be mistress of a villa, nurture babies, and all the rest. You will see," encouraged Stefano, aware that he was now trapped into pursuing the matter in earnest. He dare not again disappoint his beloved daughter—nor, for that matter, his beloved wife.

"*You* will see, my husband. You are feeding our daughter the sweet grapes of joy that will turn bitter in her mouth." Françoise quietly left the table.

Bianca thought of all the bitter grapes her mother had swallowed, but this was now, this was Bianca's life, and she was eager to savor her joy to the fullest. "We will go for the interview, will we not, Papa?" she said.

"Yes, Bianca Maria, I will confirm the time."

"Thank you, Papa," she said in triumph. "Reginoldo, will you help me select my best sketches? You have a good eye for such things."

"Of course, Bianca; it will be my pleasure."

❧

Bianca pushed all thoughts of betrothal, of Giacomo Villani, into the far corners of her mind. A second message concerning her had arrived shortly after the first—this time from Marco Biliverti. He was asking Stefano for permission to escort her to Caravaggio's studio. Still in an indulgent mood where his daughter was concerned, he had agreed—if Albret would drive them in the family carriage.

She had dressed for this occasion with the same careful attention that she had applied the first time she had anticipated meeting the artist, at the unveiling of the St. Matthew paintings. Long braids crowned her head, and her face shone with the delight of a child.

Soon she would be face to face with the great artist who had for so long been the focus of her entire being—head and heart. And dear, wonderful Marco would be her escort. Her lack of experience in the social world, especially in the company of young gentlemen, still left her ambivalent about her feelings toward him—though it mattered not, now that she was betrothed.

❧

The chilling rains of winter had returned in earnest, and Bianca was glad to have the shelter of the covered carriage. "I cannot believe I am finally going to meet Caravaggio, Marco. Thank you so much for making it possible. What do you think I should say to him?" Bianca asked nervously.

"He's a very ordinary type of person, Bianca. Tell him how you admire his paintings. He is a bit egotistical." Marco laughed. "More than a bit, actually. He brags on himself without blushing."

"Do you think he will belittle me for wanting to be an artist?"

"No, Bianca, he thinks the treatment of women in the art world is unfair."

"Well, that's true. I believe I like him for thinking that. Tell me about the 'St. John the Baptist in the Wilderness.' "

"Bianca, when you are looking at the painting, I will be looking at you—for your reaction. I don't want you to have any preconception. Just reflect your honest feelings about it."

❧

"Ah, the girl artist!" Caravaggio exclaimed as he opened the door to his studio, where Bianca stood with Marco. "Come in, come in."

"May I present Bianca Marinelli? And this is. . ." Marco had planned a little speech to introduce the artist so highly esteemed by his friend, but Caravaggio waved him aside.

"Yes, yes, I am *the* Caravaggio. Everyone knows who I am."

The simple, untidy studio fell far short of Bianca's expectations of sumptuous surroundings in a palace room. The artist's attire, though fashionable and expensive, appeared to have been worn for quite some time without benefit of laundering. In short, the great man lacked the aura of greatness. Without the courtesy of taking her hand or even pronouncing her name, he hurried her to the back of the easel.

"Stand right here, my dear; and, Marco, sit here on the low bench in your usual position. I want the girl to see both sides of the easel."

"Bi-anca," pronounced Marco, a bit disturbed by Caravaggio's manner. "The signorina's name is Bianca." He sat, blushing slightly at having to pose in front of her.

"Yes, yes, of course," said the artist. "Now, Bianca, you see what I have to work from. . . . More anguish, Marco. Drop your gaze. That's it. . . . Well, nearly. Now, Bianca, come around to the front of my canvas. . . ."

The sheepish grin faded from Marco's face as he attempted once again to portray the elusive meaning of St. John. Bianca saw only her dear friend, sitting strangely in his noble garments; the master, reduced to a quite ordinary and even boorish man; and the regal environs of her fantasy shrunk to a slovenly furnished cellar. This churl was obviously only using her as an opportunity to flaunt his own cleverness. With some resentment, she followed his direction.

Then as she stepped to the other side of the easel, her imagination could never have anticipated the awesome creation she now beheld. With an audible gasp, she clasped hands to her face. The striking painting drew forth such a surge of emotion that she stood transfixed for several moments. Never had she stood so near a large Caravaggio painting, nor had she ever been so totally enraptured.

She breathed in the smell of fresh oil paint, amazed that such greatness could be born from such commonness. Caravaggio had indeed created a St. John so human that the viewer was forced to feel his very presence and to contemplate the weight of the sorrows he bore.

But St. John the Baptist was superimposed on Marco Biliverti, his muscular body emerging from a darkened, mysterious background. His chest and legs were bare, his loins amply wrapped in camel skin, and about him was the drapery of a crimson mantle. In his right hand he held a reed cross, the only saintly attribute. The master's skill had posed him in such a manner that the left knee seemed to protrude from the canvas, bringing the figure into the viewer's space.

Most of all, though, the eyes captivated her. Marco's intense brown eyes, cast down in sorrow, revealed to Bianca the depth of a man she had dared not consider. She recalled that first time, at the Santa Suzanna, that Marco had looked at her with those eyes. She had experienced an instant thrill, but without foundation. Now that she knew his abiding faith in God, the care he took in providing for his mother and sister, his concern for others, and his enduring and encouraging friendship, she could see that Caravaggio, in his genius, had not only captured the essence of the saint, but also Marco's profound spirituality. She glanced around the easel at the flesh-and-blood Marco. In her heart the painting merged with his reality.

"Then. . .Bianca, you like my painting?" Caravaggio finally broke into her trance.

"Yes, oh yes. It is magnificent." Tears began to slide down her face. "It is too. . .wonderful."

"You think so?" said Caravaggio proudly. "Ottavio Costa thought it too wonderful for his chapel in Conscente. He is thinking of keeping it for himself at his villa and having a copy made to send to Conscente. It is a very fine painting. I believe it easily rivals my St. Matthew tableau. Do you not agree?"

"Yes, I do," she said, wiping her eyes with her handkerchief.

Marco still sat on the bench, feeling isolated from this exultation over the painting. Unaware that Bianca's emotional reaction included a realization about himself, he restrained his jealousy of Caravaggio in order to allow Bianca time with the master she so admired.

"My dear, Marco tells me you are an aspiring artist yourself. I must warn you, ladies have a most difficult time getting commissions, no matter how much talent they have—and I do believe some women can possess creative genius. But few—men or women—are able to achieve on the level of my masterpieces. And even I have been ridiculed—my commissions rejected, my genius denied."

"I know," said Bianca.

"And when you marry, well, few husbands would allow a wife to have a studio."

"I know," said Bianca.

"Wait here. I'll be right back," Caravaggio suddenly said. When he returned a few minutes later from the kitchens, he was carrying a tray with a steaming carafe, a pitcher of milk, and a few dainty pastries.

"Caffè latte," he said, pouring the two liquids into three small cups.

"Yes, I've heard of the new drink," said Marco. Bianca recalled the coffee, which she had only pretended to sample, that was served at her betrothal dinner.

Caravaggio sat on the edge of his bed and offered Bianca the one chair; Marco pulled over the low stool. In their midst Caravaggio placed the tray on a wooden crate. All agreed the coffee was interesting but would, no doubt, be a short-lived fad. The men discussed affairs of state, dueling, and other topics of little interest to Bianca.

Without preface, Caravaggio turned to Bianca and said, "I hear you have recently become betrothed to Giacomo Villani. My best wishes to the both of you."

Bianca was shocked that such news could arrive so quickly. She had hoped to keep the agreement secret from Marco for as long as possible. She thought it rude of Caravaggio to bring up the subject.

"Thank you," was all she could manage to say.

❧

As Marco assisted Bianca into the carriage, he noticed a larger, familiar-looking vehicle stationed across from the palace. He recalled having seen it stop there when they arrived earlier. "Albret," he questioned, "has that carriage remained in place while we were inside?"

"Yes, I believe it has," said Albret. "I first noticed it a few minutes after I let the two of you out. A man inside has peered out several times, as though searching for something, then retreated behind a curtain. I did, indeed, have my dagger ready."

"Oh, Albret, you are always looking for intrigue," scolded Bianca. Marco carried the conversation no further, as he was certain now that the mysterious vehicle was one from his family's carriage house in Terni. His mind, however, was preoccupied with the lovely lady beside him.

❧

Standing at the gate of the Marinelli villa, Marco took Bianca's hands in his, looked into her face, and said, "I already knew of your betrothal, Bianca. I, too, wish you only happiness."

Lowering her eyes, she answered, "It is not what I wish, but it is my duty to obey my parents." She looked back up at him. "Marco, promise to always be my friend."

"I will," said Marco, trembling with the loss of the love he had hoped to be his. A groomsman took the horses and carriage, and Marco rode off on his steed.

Albret unlocked the gate and eagerly asked about her meeting with Caravaggio.

"He's a fabulous artist. The painting of St. John is his most magnificent to date," she told him honestly. "However, the man himself is a conceited bore!" Albret shared her disappointment, as he had always delighted in gathering gossip about the famous artist for her.

But alone in her room, it was not Caravaggio who filled her thoughts. For years she had anticipated the thrill of meeting the artist. Now that she had, the event was overshadowed by the new understanding she had come to about Marco, and by a new emotion for him she dared not call—love.

fourteen

Much to Stefano's surprise, Lavinia Zapponi had found his daughter's sketches promising. Bianca admired the large biblical oil paintings in the artist's studio, especially one of Christ's resurrection, destined for a palace chapel. Lavinia was a kindly woman in her early fifties. Her children were grown, and thus she was pleased to have about her a young woman so gifted and eager to learn.

All had agreed that it was an ideal match. Bianca would live six days at Lavinia's and return to the Marinelli villa Saturday afternoon and stay through Sunday. She would be responsible for grinding and mixing pigments, stretching and preparing canvas, applying the many layers of *gesso* or sizing, and eventually executing the *imprimatura,* or initial tone, for Lavinia's designs.

As Bianca's first paintings would be on wooden panels, she would also learn to prepare and glue strips of well-seasoned poplar. All this would be tiring and tedious work, but in return, Lavinia would give her lessons in oil painting as well as supervision and the opportunity to paint alongside her.

❧

Bianca began her new life with all the enthusiasm and optimism of youth, drinking in the praise—as well as the criticism—that fueled her energy. As the weeks passed, she learned the basics quickly, deliciously immersed in the fulfillment of her dream.

One gray afternoon, as bare branches raked across the windows of the studio, Lavinia turned from her easel to Bianca, who was painstakingly transforming one of her sketches into a painted sampler for the hundredth time—or so it seemed.

"Bianca, I believe you are ready to create something more permanent. Please bring your stack of sketches."

Bianca obediently brought them, pleased finally to have arrived at a new stage. The two sat at a table by the window to benefit from the meager light, sorting and discussing the possibilities of various drawings.

"I've always been intrigued by this one," said Lavinia, "the girl in front of the obelisk, tossing crumbs into the air to the pigeons. I see you've even named it—'Essence of Joy.'"

"It is rather special," said Bianca, taking the parchment and studying it thoughtfully. That afternoon in the piazza seemed so long ago. She hadn't seen Costanza and Anabella since the festival. And Marco? Would she ever see him again? She longed to look into those brown eyes, feel the touch of his hand. Now that her "love" for Caravaggio, the man, had been greatly diminished, she knew how she felt about Marco; but alas, it was too late. It was painful to think of what might have been.

"Yes," Bianca said as she came out of her reverie, "I've imagined I might sometime—when I'm advanced enough— use it for the front panel of my *cassone*."

"That would be perfect for a *cassone!*" exclaimed Lavinia. "You could border it with spring flowers. How lovely that would be! I believe you are already advanced enough."

And so began Bianca's first real painting project. Starting with the preparation of the wood, she gave it all the care of an important altarpiece. The sketch, of course, had to be redone to fit the requirements of the chest. As the composition took shape, the drawing of Anabella matured into a young woman, remarkably similar to Bianca herself. Lavinia, like most artists in Rome, had studied the masterpieces of Caravaggio and thus was able to instruct Bianca in the foreshortening necessary to make the arms appear to reach out of the painting toward the viewer.

The *cassone* had always been a hated symbol of marriage,

a tomb for her doomed future existence. But the panel painting began to evolve into a symbol of herself, enjoying to the fullest the freedom of being who she felt she was created to be—an artist.

≈

Sometime after the installation of the painted panel on her *cassone,* Bianca was passing a Saturday afternoon at home. She and Sylvia were both engaged in needlework outside in the courtyard, where spring flowers were already beginning to emerge.

"Both your parents are quite impressed with your artistic accomplishments," said Sylvia, pausing in her work.

"Do your really think so, Sylvia? I think they find it frightening that I have already sold three paintings, including the small one of David as a shepherd boy that was bought for a chapel."

"Don't forget the two portraits you were commissioned to do."

"Yes, but I really don't count portraits. They are the traditional subjects for women. To me, a real painting tells a story," said Bianca, as a smile stole across her face. "I imagine when a woman poses for a portrait that she is my model. It gives me a chance to really study and reproduce facial features."

"Yes, I understand women are not allowed to draw from real people—except for portraits."

"Isn't that ridiculous, Sylvia? But hands are what most interest me. Sometimes Lavinia will position her hands for me to sketch. The male figure is difficult, also, and, as it is unacceptable to stare at men, I can gain very little through observation. I do still study Caravaggio's paintings, however. I may have misjudged him the one time we met. Boor that he was, he is still the greatest artist of all time, in my opinion. Surely there is a depth of soul to create as he does."

"So you still think he is your true love?"

"No. . .no, my love belongs to someone else."

"Giacomo?"

"Surely you jest, Sylvia. My heart will never belong to old Fork-Beard."

⋙

True to his promise, Stefano had diligently sought occasions to bring Bianca and Giacomo together. However, the young man had never found it convenient for them to meet in Florence, and the months had passed with only one brief visit in Rome. Unannounced, he had arrived one Sunday morning and accompanied the family to church. Naturally, he was invited to spend the remainder of the day at the Marinelli villa. Bianca's opinion of her betrothed did not improve during the afternoon in which the four played several hands of cards.

Giacomo had planned to spend a week attending to various details at the bank, then calling on Bianca each afternoon. However, when he learned at the close of the card playing that she was spending her weekdays at an artist's studio, he became sullen and showed his disapproval by refusing to visit her at all. For her part, Bianca was hardly distressed at this punishment but feared that he might soon demand an end to her studies.

⋙

On that momentous visit to Caravaggio's studio, Bianca had told Marco of her upcoming interview with Lavinia Zapponi. He had prayed that this dream might be fulfilled for her. In fact, the lovely, intriguing Bianca was almost constantly in his thoughts, but he made no move to see her out of respect for the betrothal. He grieved not only for his own loss, but also over the knowledge that it was not what she wished for herself. From time to time he passed the Piazza del Popolo in hopes of a mere stolen glimpse of her. But alas, she was pursuing her dream elsewhere.

After modeling for Caravaggio, Marco had gone a couple of weeks without income. The needlework pieces that Costanza and Anabella were able to sell in the marketplace barely paid for food. Fortunately, just as poor weather was driving away their customers, the architect Carlo Maderno sought out Marco to assist in measuring and studying the present St. Peter's Basilica in preparation for the enlargement.

Another great concern was for his lost seignoiry. The Bishop Ferrante had indicated that it might be two or three months before he would return from his journey to Perugia, with a stop in his home town of Terni. Surely he would hear from him shortly.

In the meantime he was disturbed that Jacopo might be living in Rome. He had actually seen him in the procession at the Fall Festival, when their eyes had met. Since then he had suspected that Jacopo was following him. In addition to the incident of the carriage at the Palazzo Madama, he thought he had seen him on another occasion, lurking behind some bushes. As the time to prepare the vineyards approached, he also worried that without proper supervision, the estate— built with such care by his father—might fall into ruin.

❧

Bianca's talent blossomed. Since the quality of her work was apparent, and yet she was unable at this early stage to command large sums, commissions began to come to her—especially for small, private chapels. One was for a painting of Jesus sitting at a table in the home of Zacchaeus, the tax collector. Recalling another painting of a tax collector, St. Matthew, Bianca asked Albret to stop the carriage on her weekly return home, at the San Luigi dei Francesi. She entered to pray for wisdom in creating the biblical scene and to once again study from the master.

Outside, Albret descended from the carriage to stroll and pick up any news he might hear. This was always a good environment for gossip of Caravaggio—and that so pleased Bianca—since the French church stood next to the Palazzo Madama. A small crowd was forming around a man who was telling of a recent murder.

With casual interest, Albret approached. The man, in a loud voice, was proclaiming, ". . .and even with that help, the man died. According to these friends, it seems the argument was over a wager they had made about their game of tennis. Caravaggio has fled the city, as well he should. He knows—save an unlikely pardon from the state—that he will be condemned to death."

Caravaggio! Albret's interest peaked. "*Signore,* who was the unfortunate tennis partner?" he boldly asked.

"Runccio or something like that," furnished one gentleman.

"Ranuccio Tomassoni," said another. "They often played tennis together and wagered on the score."

"He stabbed him in the thigh, he did, without mercy," a man in dark attire, who seemed to be enjoying the gore, added.

"Did he come back to his studio before escaping?" someone asked the bearer of news.

"No one at the palace seems to know. However, according to one who often visited there, several of his paintings on rolled-up canvas are missing."

"Could have been stolen," the dark-attired gentleman interjected.

The crowd began to disperse, as no more news seemed to be forthcoming. Albret felt this last gentleman staring in his direction, and thus kept an eye on him as they both headed back toward their carriages. He was thin, somewhat hunched, and wore the gold embossed doublet of a Spanish nobleman. His black beard came to a sharp point, as did the two parts of his mustache. Albret was certain the man stepped into the same carriage Marco had once asked him about.

Bianca emerged from the church, radiant and joyful from prayer and study of the paintings. "Oh, Albret, I do so feel that God has granted me the ability to paint to His glory," she said, hopping into the waiting carriage. "Marco used to tell me how Caravaggio always wanted to make the Scriptures meaningful to all people. That is how I feel, Albret." She turned to him enthusiastically, then saw the distress on his young face.

"What is it, Albret?"

"It is with a heavy heart that I must tell you the news I have just learned—about Caravaggio." With that introduction he told her every word he had heard as accurately as possible.

Bianca was stunned. How could this possibly be true? A man who paints to God's glory, and whom God has blessed with such insight and talent, could not conceivably commit murder in cold blood. She pressed her hands to her temples, trying to stop the dizziness.

"Albret!" she suddenly exclaimed. "This is not the Via Margutta. Where are you going?"

"Stay calm, Bianca," he whispered. "I think—but I'm not sure—that a carriage is following us. Perhaps we can lose him if I go through the marketplace." With that news, Bianca sobbed uncontrollably.

"Now, now—don't cry." Albret was unaccustomed to weeping ladies and felt more awkward with his charge than he did in escaping from the stalker. By weaving in and out among the carriages in the congested market and by taking a few sharp turns, he felt confident they were no longer being pursued.

fifteen

"Bianca, you have progressed remarkably, especially in this last painting that you have called 'Zacchaeus, Contrite before the Master.' I believe you could be classed as one of the Caravaggisti—or, rather, as the lone Caravaggista. But why have you shone the light on Zacchaeus and painted only the back of Jesus?" said Paolo, Lavinia's husband. He was securing the new painting in an elaborate frame, as Lavinia and Bianca watched.

Bianca felt the previously coveted word *Caravaggista* fall hollow. She chose instead to respond to the second part of his comment: "To me, most portrayals of Jesus seem to fall short. I really believe He cannot be adequately painted as a person—even though He actually was a man as well as God. For that reason I believe it best to have His face hidden, and leave it to the viewer to supply the Jesus in his heart. It is, however, Jesus' light that is reflected on the face of Zacchaeus. That is the best I can do."

"I didn't mean it as criticism, Bianca. I was just curious. I accept your explanation," said Paolo, who was an artist in his own right, though he spent most of his time framing paintings for Lavinia and others. "There, how do you like it in this frame?"

"It's fabulous!" exclaimed Lavinia. The couple had become like second parents to Bianca. She was at ease in their company but seldom shared her feelings with them.

"As my husband says, you have progressed phenomenally, just with this painting. The emotion—the contriteness—on the face of Zacchaeus. . . What's so extraordinary is that you are barely seventeen and already have such depth in your perception of feeling. I didn't begin to show such emotion in my figures until well into my forties—after many of life's hard experiences."

Bianca smiled and thanked them both for their praise. *It's my sadness over the downfall of Caravaggio,* she thought. Then she questioned, *Where is God's hand in all of this? Did He have a part at all in Caravaggio's genius? Was his painting to the glory of God all a sham? Is my painting all a sham that will come to nothing? Have I only imagined that God has given me a gift and prepared my way?*

❧

The grief that burdened Bianca made her feel as if a large part of her life had disappeared. The romantic love for the imagined man had faded with that first meeting, but she had held on to her belief of the divine inspiration of his work. She tried to pray for answers to her questions, but, as there seemed to be no response from God, she began to question even her faith. She needed to talk to a friend. Where was Marco? She missed him terribly. Painting was the only solace for the sadness of her soul.

In the midst of this confusion, her greatest opportunity came. All of her commissions had been completed, and she had just stepped into the studio with the thought of beginning something of her own choosing. She heard Lavinia running up the stairs, calling her name. "Bianca," she said again breathlessly as she entered. "Bianca, you have a most important-looking letter, just delivered. It's doubtlessly a very fine commission."

Bianca broke the seal and read aloud: "You have been selected to compete, along with two other artists, to paint the altarpiece for the Chiesa Nuova. The undersigned committee has reviewed your work and was especially drawn to the 'Zacchaeus, Contrite before the Master.' We stipulate that this piece be a biblical narrative of your choosing, but it must include Jesus Christ with at least one other figure. These are the required dimensions. . ."

"Oh, Bianca, how wonderful!" exclaimed her tutor. "What an honor for one so young!"

"I don't know," said Bianca, rather dazed. "I will not attempt to paint the face of Jesus. And what does this mean, 'along with two other artists'?"

"Such competitions are rather common. Three artists are selected to do a work, then the winning painting is purchased. But it is a great honor to be asked to compete. It confirms you as a recognized artist, and even if your painting is not the one selected, it will bring a high price simply because of your new status. I am so proud of my student!" said Lavinia with sincere emotion.

"I will consider it," said Bianca, beginning to comprehend the importance of this opportunity. "I've never done a painting as large as the one they want." *This is Marco's church,* Bianca recalled to herself. *I wonder if he knows about this?*

❧

Indeed Marco *had* learned that the three competing artists included Bianca Marinelli. From the committee members he also learned the location of Lavinia's home and studio. Surely it would not be indiscreet to call on Bianca just once and take her a small gift as a token of his congratulations. *She has probably heard the awful story of Caravaggio,* he thought. *Perhaps she would like to share her disappointment with a friend.*

❧

Bianca felt herself at a spiritual crossroads. Her questions that the crime of Caravaggio brought to mind enlarged and encompassed all her religious beliefs. She recalled her mother's story of how her grandfather—whom she had never known—had been put to death for an obvious act of kindness. Why hadn't this powerful God saved him?

Pushed by Lavinia and her husband to enter the contest, she agreed. In one afternoon she completed a sketch of Mary Magdalene recognizing Jesus at his tomb on Easter morning.

By adapting the image that had begun as Anabella tossing crumbs, then evolving into herself with uplifted arms on the *cassone*, the pose was now transformed into the Magdalene worshiping the Christ. She placed Jesus at the left, standing with his back to the viewer. For such an important work she would make a smaller study to test the colors and composition.

❧

On a pleasant day in spring, Lavinia opened her gate to a young man who had come to visit briefly with her student. She welcomed him into her sitting room to determine the purpose of his visit.

"I am a friend of Bianca's, and I have come to congratulate her on being asked to compete for the Chiesa Nuova altarpiece. You see, that is my church. The entire fellowship is eager to know the results. I have nothing to do with the judging, but want merely to encourage her and wish her well," said Marco straightforwardly.

Lavinia dutifully questioned him on his background and the length of his friendship with Bianca. "And have you seen much of her work?" she asked.

"Only a remarkable sketch of a twisted olive tree," said Marco, recalling the circumstances of that encounter. "Of course, I would love to see her paintings. I'm sure you have taught her much."

"Unfortunately, none of them are at the studio at present, but *she* is, preparing a canvas for a study. It will serve as a sort of practice piece before creating the large one for the competition," Lavinia said graciously. "Wait here, and I will ask if the lady wishes to see you." Marco sat, twisting his damp palms together. He wondered if Bianca would even want to see him.

Lavinia returned bearing the news Marco was hoping to hear.

When Marco at last entered the studio, Bianca's face shone radiantly.

"Marco, it is so good to see you." She beamed.

You are even more beautiful than I remembered, thought Marco. "It is a delight to be here. I have come to congratulate you on being asked to enter the competition. Is this the sketch for the painting?"

"Yes, do you like it?" said Bianca, handing him the parchment and suddenly feeling shy.

"Like it? Bianca, it is wonderful. I love the pose of Mary Magdalene."

"It was inspired by a sketch I made of Anabella. That's when I met your sister and mother for the first time."

Marco held the parchment and studied every detail, as if he wished not to give it up. He looked back at Bianca and saw a woman who had matured in character and grace of movement; she was more self-composed than he remembered.

"Here, I will make it a gift to you." She took the parchment, wrote "To my friend, Marco," then signed and dated it. "I will need it a few more days for the study, then I will have Albret take it to your home—wherever that is."

They both laughed, for as long as they had known each other, she had never been to his house. Marco wrote his street and directions on a scrap of parchment that was lying on the table. "Thank you, Bianca. I shall treasure this always." Then with a grin, he added, "Perhaps some day, when you are famous, it will be worth a tidy sum."

"My husband can set it in a simple frame for you," said a glowing Lavinia, wanting to be a part of this happiness.

A thousand subjects that Marco wanted to discuss with Bianca whirled about in his head, but he felt it was not proper to stay. "I must take my leave now. Thank you, Lavinia, for your hospitality."

"But my dear Marco," said Lavinia, "I was about to propose an idea I had. It is a lovely day, and Bianca has been downcast of late. Why don't you take her riding to the old ruins. You can borrow one of our horses, Bianca. Now, don't disappoint me by refusing."

After only moderate reluctance, for propriety's sake, the two agreed.

~

The ride out to the old Roman Forum was invigorating. They passed the Castle of Sant'Angelo and crossed the Tiber on the ancient, statue-flanked bridge. Bianca sat regally in her sidesaddle on a fine dappled mare. She wore a light cape over a dress that matched the deep blue of the sky. Her dark curls tumbled loosely from under her riding hat.

Marco's chestnut steed pranced with excitement as they reached the other side of the bridge and followed the path along the river. Marco had difficulty keeping him from pulling ahead of the other horse. Wayward locks framed Marco's handsome face, and his noble attire—though beginning to fray—left no doubt that here was a man of distinction who knew well his own mind.

When they reached a wide, grassy plain, Bianca urged her horse into a gallop, passing Marco with peals of laughter. He quickly caught up, and the two raced as carefree as the wind until their destination drew them into a narrow street.

"I've not been here since I was a little girl," said Bianca, out of breath from the gallop. "Papa brought my brothers and me here and tried in vain to teach us a little history."

"I came here with my parents, also, before Anabella was born. I'm sure I questioned them endlessly about every stone," said Marco in a mocking boast.

"You did not," Bianca chuckled.

"Well, maybe I asked what those tall columns were doing standing out there by themselves, not holding up anything at all," Marco said as they entered the area of the old Roman Forum.

"I think this is where you decided to be a stonemason," she teased.

They dismounted and tied their horses to saplings. The

area was dotted with the yellow and purple of wildflowers, nodding in the breeze. Shrubbery grew from the tops of decaying structures, and a fern hugged a toppled capital— giving the place an eerie ambiance of passing time.

Bianca ran, fleet as a delighted child, to the group of useless columns. She stood like a Roman goddess among them, her blue dress billowing to the side. As the cape grew warm in the sun, she loosened the tie and let it slip off to fall across her arm. She began humming one of her mother's French folk songs, as free and happy as the wild orchids at her feet.

Marco sat on the fallen capital and gazed at this ephemeral, slender figure. How comely and talented she was! He ached with the knowledge that she was pledged to another.

Bianca walked slowly back to him, spread her cape on the capital, and seated herself next to him. "Marco, did you hear about Caravaggio?" she asked, becoming serious.

"Yes—yes, and I immediately thought about how it would hurt you."

"I don't understand how a man like him could murder someone."

"From what I hear, it was an accident. He and Tomassoni often drew swords in sport. There were three or four friends who witnessed it all."

"An accident? I didn't know."

"Tomassoni accused Caravaggio of cheating—they had wagers on the game. Some say he did cheat, others that he didn't, but all the witnesses agree that Tomassoni attacked first. He cut his ear and sliced across his neck."

Bianca winced.

"Perhaps I am telling you too much."

"No, no, go on. I'm glad to know it was not a cold-blooded murder. I need to know the details."

"Caravaggio stabbed his partner in the thigh. Or he may have fallen on him and stabbed him accidentally. That part is vague. The friends tried to stop the bleeding but to no avail.

While they were doing so, Caravaggio fled. That was a big mistake. He might have received a pardon from the state, but now. . ."

"Do you think Caravaggio really loved God and painted for his glory, so people could better understand the Scriptures? I worry about this. It has shaken my faith."

"Bianca, we all have faults; we have all sinned. I withheld from you what I knew about his quick temper. He had been in trouble with the law before. You admired him so much, I didn't want to change that for you."

"Oh, Marco, please don't be like my parents. Promise never again to withhold information from me—for my protection."

"I promise. I see now that it only made this harder for you. But don't let it interfere with your faith. God is good. He is a loving Father who forgives all who come to Him. He will forgive Caravaggio even now, if he will ask Him. I believe God blessed him with a talent, and he chose to use it for God. That was a choice. Like all of us, he made some bad choices, too. I think he enjoyed risk."

"I looked up to Caravaggio and thought he was perfect—because he painted so perfectly," she confessed. "Before I met him that day with you, Marco, I really believed I loved him. In the flesh he seemed so rude and self-absorbed. But his painting seems to be on a higher level than he is, don't you think so, Marco?"

"There is something extraordinary about his paintings. God has used him to get a holy message across because Caravaggio had given his talent to God. Maybe he hasn't given over his anger to God—so that he can be healed. I don't mean to judge. . ."

"Marco, I love talking with you. I am so often deceived by my own emotions, but somehow you always are able to unscramble things and make them clear."

"Well, I try," Marco said, somewhat embarrassed by her praise. "But I am concerned about how this has shaken your faith. Just remember that the messages of Caravaggio's paintings are just as true today as they were before. . .that event. And God has not changed one bit. In fact, He may be speaking through your work just as He has through Caravaggio's. Don't you think God had a hand in making your training possible?"

Bianca nodded, but began to sob quietly. With the truth so evident, her doubting seemed ungrateful. Marco instinctively wrapped his strong arms around her and held her close. The sobbing increased, and she trembled with heartrending emotion. "There, there," he whispered, sliding his fingers through her silky hair. The bittersweetness of his love for her tore at his heart. Only God could work a miracle that would allow him to act on that love. Then he felt the tension of her body relax.

He lightly kissed her forehead. Her red-blotched face turned up to his, and she smiled. The two sat motionless for several seconds; then he released his arms from around her.

"I promised to no longer withhold information from you," he said. "I have some news that may turn out to be good. About recovering my property."

"Wonderful! I would love to know what is happening in that regard," she answered, regaining her composure.

"The Bishop Ferrante has sent me a verbal message by his page," said Marco. "I had sought his help after learning that he often supported a younger brother's right to inheritance. He spent two days on my behalf while he was in Terni recently.

"He is convinced that Jacopo has spread false rumors about me. Also, he has learned that many of the workers whom my father employed are now begging on the streets. Jacopo is doing nothing to ready the vineyards—the vines have not been pruned nor has the ground been tilled. In short, Bishop Ferrante plans to draw up a document stating these matters and to put pressure on him to do what is right without forcing him into court. Unfortunately, the bishop has many other matters before him, and I do not foresee him acting soon."

"But, at least he is taking your side. He has the power to force the issue, does he not?"

"Yes, but if he doesn't act soon, I may try something else. I cannot abide waiting for another."

"What could you do?"

"I could go to the castle at a time when I know Jacopo is away, take command, and, with the loyal servants, fight him off as an intruder when he returns."

"Would there not be bloodshed?"

"Probably. Of course, I could not be sure that the servants would fight on my side. They might be loyal to him. Also, from the bishop I learned that Jacopo is in residence at Terni at present. But I have seen him at least once—and perhaps three times—here in Rome. Do you remember, Bianca, a man who was watching us from another carriage as we left Caravaggio's studio?"

"Yes, but I thought nothing of it at the time," she said as she put two events together. "I'm sure it was the same carriage that followed Albret and me the afternoon we found out about Caravaggio. We finally lost him in the marketplace. He was your brother?"

"Half brother. I'm sorry he frightened you," Marco said. "Well, anyhow, I have the beginning of a plan. Do you have any ideas?"

Bianca laughed. "Certainly not a battle plan. Maybe you could outwit him somehow. Please, I don't want there to be violence."

"Nor do I. Thank you for reminding me. I was just speaking out of frustration. At the fellowship I hear a great deal about God's perfect timing. I know the right thing to do at this point is to trust God with the outcome. Surely I will hear from the bishop again soon."

The two strolled through the ruins, inventing silly stories of what might have happened there in times past. Marco picked a bouquet of wild, purple orchids and presented them to Bianca on bended knee, as if he were a knight of yore. "These are as fragrant and beautiful as you, milady," he said in a mock tone to cover his earnestness.

Then they each brought the other up to date on their daily routines—Marco about his work at St. Peter's, Bianca about her new life with Lavinia and her husband and how painting was replete with the expected joy. All too soon the lengthening shadows reminded them it was time to ride back into reality, leaving the sweetness of this afternoon for each to cherish in memory.

As they approached the grazing horses, Marco said, "Bianca, I almost forgot that I brought you something—a small gift to congratulate you on the competition." He reached into his saddlebag. "Close your eyes and I will place it in your hands."

When she opened her eyes, she discovered a delicately designed case of *cloisonné* on gold background. Lifting the ornate lid, she discovered that the box was lined in red velvet.

"It's exquisite, Marco. Thank you," she said.

"I thought you could put your keepsakes in it. Mother sells these for a man she knows from the church fellowship. I thought you might like it."

"I do. Very much," she whispered. As she held the small case, Marco clasped his hands around hers. They looked deep into each other's eyes, silently communicating the love that they both recognized. Without words, they sealed a pledge of eternal love—though desire must always remain denied.

sixteen

Lavinia was pleased that the ride had cheered Bianca. Her cheeks were flushed and her hair awry upon her return, but it was evident that her mood had improved considerably. "The ruins are incredible," Bianca announced. "One is so aware of the passing of time." But after only a brief, polite conversation, Bianca rushed up to her little sleeping room off the studio. There she carefully pressed between the pages of a book the precious bunch of purple orchids. *These are a treasure more valuable than jewels,* she thought to herself, *for they were given me by my only true love.* Later, she would place them in the *cloisonné* case he had given her for keepsakes.

Then she knelt beside her bed and poured her heart out to God. She asked forgiveness for doubting her Lord and promised to trust Him more. She prayed for Marco, that his property would be restored. She prayed for God's help in creating her entry for the altarpiece.

But, although Marco had helped her understand much about God, Caravaggio, and herself, he had stirred up another question that she dared not ask him: If God's timing were so perfect, why had He failed to enable Marco to regain his property and become eligible to marry her *before* her hated betrothal to Giacomo?

੨੩

The painting for the altarpiece was not going well. Bianca had not quite completed the study before she began work on the larger canvas. "The composition is correct. So is line and color," said Lavinia, appraising the work. "The extended arms of Mary Magdalene are even more realistic than in the figure on your *cassone.* But I agree, Bianca. It lacks passion."

"Her face is the problem," groaned Bianca. "I cannot get it right. That is why I could not finish the study. And we must present it to the committee one week from today."

"What are you trying to show?"

"I—I guess I don't really know," said Bianca, startled at the realization that she had no goal.

"There is a Holy Bible on the stand in the library. You will find the passage you are illustrating near the end of the book of St. John. Drink in every word of it, and I believe you will find what is lacking." Lavinia patted her shoulder with understanding. "Illustrating a story from the Bible has an added dimension—a divine purpose. I find I must read the passage to fully understand it, and I pray before painting."

≈

Marco hung the framed sketch in his bedroom and stood back to determine its straightness. "To my friend, Marco," he read aloud. He studied the script, so precise, yet free—a natural preciseness, like Bianca. Albret had brought it to the house that afternoon, while he was away working at the Basilica.

Anabella had been so excited when he came home, her words tumbled all over each other. He couldn't tell if she was more enthusiastic over the drawing or over Albret. Marco remembered Albret as an awkward, gangly youth with unsightly fuzz on his chin. To hear his sister describe him, he was "tall and handsome, with a charming little beard."

"Albret told me Bianca drew the Magdalene after me. When I posed for her by the obelisk. But there's no obelisk, and I'm grown up in this drawing." She had babbled nonstop while Marco tried to look at the sketch.

Now he had it all to himself, but he chuckled at his sister's remarks. Soon she would be grown up. Albret was an intelligent, well-mannered lad, and he liked him. But he was a servant, hardly the prince 'Bella aspired to marry. He wondered about himself. How could he ever marry anyone—besides Bianca Marinelli.

⅏

Bianca crept into the library early the next morning. The marble floor felt cool to her bare feet. She had hardly slept, worrying about the painting. What if it was not even good, and they mocked her ineptness? Lavinia had been able to find out a great deal about the Chiesa Nuova. Because the fellowship had grown so rapidly, they had been forced to build this second building. She also heard that Peter Paul Rubens had been commissioned to do three paintings in the chancel. A wealthy Flemish artist, he had recently come to Rome, where he was receiving high acclaim. "You don't want yours to seem pale next to his brilliant colors," Lavinia had cautioned. The more she learned, the more intimidated she became. *Who am I to do this work?* she questioned.

Bianca set her candle on a stand next to the large Bible. She fingered the book with reverence. Few people owned Bibles—her family certainly didn't—and people were not generally encouraged to do private reading. She had only seen one high on the altar on a huge lectern, and it was read by a priest. Was it even right for her to touch it? Yet Marco had told her how, at their fellowship, they met in small groups and studied the Scriptures together. That's where he learned that God was truly loving and forgiving, not willing that any should perish.

Now, where was the book of St. John? Since it concerned Jesus, it would be in the New Testament. The stories about Mary Magdalene were familiar from the church readings. *Ah, here is what I am looking for.* Near the end of the book she found the account of Christ's resurrection and Mary Magdalene's finding his empty tomb:

> Thinking he was the gardener, she said, "Sir, if you have carried him away, tell me where you have put him, and I will get him."
> Jesus said to her, "Mary." She turned toward him and cried out in Aramaic, "Rabboni!" (which means Teacher).

Having never read the words for herself, this was a mystical and spiritual experience. She thought of how Mary Magdalene had come early in the morning to bring spices to the tomb. What would that have been like? She breathed in deeply and closed her eyes. She felt the presence of Jesus before her. In her mind she heard her name, *Bianca.* Aloud, she whispered, "Teacher, what would you have me do?"

The trust that she had promised her Lord engulfed her without any effort on her part. She realized now that all she had needed to do was to be *willing* to trust. Reading further, she noted that Jesus had told Mary Magdalene to go tell His disciples that He had risen. When she found them, she exclaimed, "I have seen the Lord!"

Bianca knelt and whispered with a new kind of joy that she had never known before, "Thank you, Lord Jesus, for revealing Yourself to me." She experienced a new freedom, the kind that can't be taken away even by the bars of a prison—or by an unwanted marriage. The love of God was a certainty that could not be shaken by human events.

She rose from her epiphany and hurried into the studio. In a near frenzy she mixed her paints. The dress became a vivid blue on the half-kneeling Mary Magdalene. She ran to the window and watched the morning sunlight brush the tips of leaves on the vegetation below. She noticed how shafts of light burst between the trunks of trees, how rocks were crowned in golden light at the same time that they cast dark shadows.

Rushing back to her easel, she reproduced these natural phenomena with the twisted olive trees and rock-hewn tomb. But Jesus Christ was the source of light, his back in shadow. The face of Mary Magdalene reflected the light of her Savior. Bianca must make that face show the impact of His love, His forgiveness. *Lord, guide my hand,* she prayed. The eyes of her subject turned upward, the lips parted in awe. The face showed more than surprise. It revealed understanding.

She named her work "I Have Seen the Lord!"

seventeen

The three competing paintings hung on separate walls of the narthex in the Chiesa Nuova. Marco immediately recognized the one by Bianca, as it matched the sketch he so treasured. The enormity of the paintings startled him. He stood a few moments in front of each of the other two entries. In his judgment, they were both excellent. But then who was he to judge? He knew so little about art. Several people he had never seen at the fellowship wandered from picture to picture, giving their opinions to whoever would listen. Finally, stationing himself before the one he had come to view, he was amazed at its emotional impact. To his untrained eye, it easily ranked up there with Caravaggio's work.

But he was not alone in his high opinion. Two others, both of whom seemed knowledgeable, were discussing it.

"I say no woman could have painted with such genius," said one, rubbing his chin.

"It certainly grips the viewer. It's masterfully done," said his companion.

"I'm amazed they invited a woman to compete."

"She's a total unknown. Competitions such as this are usually reserved for the very best. Even Rubens was not invited."

"But he has been commissioned for some of the paintings. How could this girl's work hang next to his? That is, if she is actually the artist."

Marco felt his heart sink. "Pardon me, *signori,* but I am acquainted with the artist, and know of a certainty that this is, indeed, her own work."

"You don't say?" said one of the men. They both bowed slightly and left, mumbling to each other.

Marco was well-acquainted with one of the lay priests on the committee. He could often be found in a church office, where he counseled and prayed with those in spiritual need. Fortunately, Marco found him there alone, studying.

"Guido, my good man, may I have a brief word with you?"

"Certainly, Marco. What is on your mind?"

"I was just looking at the three paintings competing for our altarpiece. . . ."

"Yes, yes, aren't they magnificent? Our judges will have a difficult task. Whichever they choose, there will be disgruntled parishioners, don't you think?"

"No doubt," said Marco. "But my concern at the moment is a conversation I just overheard. Two men were expressing their opinion about the artist, Bianca Marinelli. They questioned her authorship because they believed no woman was capable of such great art."

"Go on," encouraged Guido.

"Well, I was concerned that such rumors might find their way to the ears of the committee. I just wanted to assure you that I can attest to the fact that it is solely her work."

Guido leaned back in his chair with a friendly chuckle. "No need to worry, my friend. Such rumors have been spinning around since the painting was first put on view over a week ago. As you know, all three artists were invited to participate because they were relatively unknown. There are two advantages for us: The prize money can be low, and we have the opportunity to be the first to recognize a potential luminary. The works of all three were studied arduously by those more keen in such matters than I."

"So you will not be swayed by such nonsense?"

"The final decision will be made by three judges from a different parish."

"But, what if. . ."

"We have even sent a representative to the young lady's tutor, Lavinia Zapponi. Some have suggested that she is the

true artist who painted the figures, and that Signorina Marinelli merely did the background. The tutor claims she resisted
even making the slightest brush stroke and offered her a minimum of advice. Our greatest proof is in a comparison of
styles. Though, of course, there is some similarity between
teacher and student, the manner is strikingly different—especially concerning the use of light and the facial expression of
Mary Magdalene."

"But Lavinia Zapponi is herself a woman. . . ."

"Yes, and those who claim her as the author prejudge
Signorina Marinelli for her *youth*. On the other hand, many
who discredit her because of her gender are saying the painting could be the work of Caravaggio. The style is truly more
like his, but he is the last person on earth who would permit
another to sign his work. Besides, he has left the city. Therefore, we on the committee are not in the least concerned.
However, thank you for your added assurance."

Marco left the church with more alarm than ever. The
rumors were much more widespread than he had imagined.
Even if the committee and the judges discounted them, they
could continue long after the competition—*especially* if she
were to win.

❧

Bianca had decided to take some time away from the studio.
Finishing the painting, and the spiritual awakening that
accompanied the feat, had drained her energies. Total
strangers who had seen her painting came by the studio to
praise her work. Three commissions had resulted. Now, she
looked forward to the usual quiet of the Marinelli villa.

In the carriage on the way home, Albret alerted her to a different situation that awaited her arrival. Not only had well-
wishers come by the villa nearly nonstop, but the Gentileschis
had been invited to dinner that evening.

"They will be entertaining," said Bianca, enlivened somewhat by the thought of pleasant company. "Artemisia and I

always enjoy each other's company."

"And there is someone else who will be there. . . ." Albret drew in a long breath, glanced at Bianca, and finished his sentence: "Giacomo."

Bianca sat up straight in the carriage. "No, I don't want to see him! When did he arrive? He is not staying long, I hope."

"Bianca, I knew you wouldn't be pleased, but he arrived three days ago—and he is staying in Roberto's room."

"Roberto's room! Why? His room has not been used since—since he died. Why not Reginoldo's room?"

"Because," Albret explained as though speaking to a young child, "Reginoldo will be here, also, for the dedication of your painting at Chiesa Nuova—if you win."

"But surely Fork-Beard will be gone by then!"

"I don't like bearing all the bad news, but your father has invited him to stay for the ceremonies. He is certain you will win. But, even if not, he is concerned that the two of you are not getting to know each other, and this presents an opportunity."

"I see," said Bianca. She remained quiet the rest of the journey. A hot tear slid down her cheek. She felt Marco's warm hands resting over hers as she held his little gift. *Oh, Marco, hold me. You should be the one waiting for me at the villa. . . .*

૨ે.

The praise embarrassed Bianca. Though proud of her achievements, she was not accustomed to having so much attention directed toward her. She found it difficult to respond to compliments and often was at a loss as to how to answer the many questions.

At dinner, all attempts at other topics of conversation died quickly. Giacomo tried in vain to interject a word on banking to Stefano, but the adoring father was relishing every word of praise heaped on his daughter.

"I propose a toast," offered Orazio Gentileschi. "To the first Caravaggista. May her acclaim put to rest forever the outrageous notion that women cannot achieve on the same level as men."

"You speak in truth, my good man," said Stefano, who was so caught up in the moment that he relented a small measure in his long-held belief.

"I'm so pleased for you," said Artemisia without the slightest hint of jealousy.

Françoise twisted her napkin.

Giacomo helped himself to another serving of ravioli.

❧

Following dinner, Giacomo succeeded in engaging Stefano in a banking discussion. Bianca snatched this opportunity to slip off to her room with Artemisia.

"Tell me, Artemisia, how your artwork is progressing," said Bianca as she settled on her bed, leaving the chair for her friend.

"I've sold a few portraits of women and children. Father believes that is a good place to begin, but he is teaching me elements of composition for narrative pieces. He is really very captivated by your 'I Have Seen the Lord.' He took me to see it yesterday. I found it remarkable. Many others were also admiring it."

"And saying a girl couldn't possibly have done it?"

"I didn't know if you knew. . ."

"Didn't know if I knew if someone else really painted it?" Bianca giggled.

"As a girl, you would be too stupid to know if you did it or not!" retorted Artemisia, continuing the sarcasm.

They both howled. Bianca buried her face in her pillow. Laughing so outrageously, she was afraid of being heard downstairs. Her head began to throb in pain, but this light moment was too delicious to pass up.

Suddenly Artemisia noticed the *cassone.* "Did you paint that panel, Bianca?" she asked in complete seriousness. "The woman resembles the Mary Magdalene of your painting."

"I thought I did, but perhaps it was someone else."

Again the girls burst into uncontrollable laughter. Artemisia found a cushion in which to stifle her merriment, and Bianca clung to her own pillow.

When at last calm prevailed, they found much to talk seriously about. But, of course, Caravaggio was their most intense subject. Bianca shared the details she had heard from Marco, and Artemisia told that he had been spotted in Naples, suffering from a fever caused by his wounds. Bianca pressed her fingers to her temples in an effort to arrest the throbbing.

A knock at the door brought an end to this pleasure in friendship. Sylvia announced that the Gentileschi family was leaving, and that Françoise had requested that Bianca come downstairs.

"Please tell Mother I suffer from a headache and the exhaustion of the past week. And make it known to Signor and Signora Gentileschi that it was a delight to have them in our home, and I thank them for all their kind remarks."

Sylvia nodded and returned with Bianca's messages.

Bianca lay back on her bed, exhausted. "Thanks for being here, Artemisia. I treasure your friendship."

"And I yours," said Artemisia, squeezing her hand. "Do you really have a headache?"

"I do, but who wouldn't after all our silliness? And I truly am exhausted, but I'm so glad you came."

At the door Artemisia turned back and whispered, "Don't let any more men sign your name to their paintings." They both had a final snicker, and she was gone.

❧

Bianca's headache worsened. In the morning she asked Sylvia to draw the draperies across the windows, as the light seemed blinding. She remained in bed, too nauseous to eat. Françoise hovered over her, concerned about how her illness would be perceived—that perchance it was due to her penetrating an endeavor for which women are not emotionally constituted.

By midmorning the headache had passed, and Bianca felt well enough to come downstairs and partake of some nourishment. As she nibbled at her bread, Françoise made an effort at cheerfulness. "Giacomo has been so worried about you, Bianca. He paced the floor continuously yesterday, so deep was his concern. He awaits you now in the sitting room."

Bianca dutifully went to him. She found him engaged in a lively conversation with her father. Pausing at the door, she heard Stefano say, "Your rise in the financial world is certainly to be admired, my son."

Immediately both men rose to welcome her. As all three took chairs, Stefano exclaimed with enthusiasm. "Giacomo's life experiences are so like my own, Bianca Maria. We both were nurtured by hard-working farm families. And we both were fortunate enough to be recommended for apprenticeships at the Medici bank in Florence. Thus we have risen in the banking business, but he far swifter than I."

Bianca gave a smile of acknowledgment.

"Ladies have no interest in such topics, however," said Giacomo with an air of superiority.

"Then I shall leave the two of you to discuss whatever pleases you both," said Stefano, graciously taking his leave.

No sooner had her father left than Giacomo leaned forward in his chair, his hands gripping the chair arms. Bianca thought he looked like a cat ready to spring. She laced her fingers in anticipation.

"I am not at all pleased with this painting business," he began with restrained irritation. "It is not at all proper. This competing openly reflects poorly on me, your betrothed. Be advised that this foolishness will all end the day we become husband and wife."

Before Bianca could utter a word, Albret entered. With a slight bow and a twinkle in his eye, he announced: "I have a message here from the Chiesa Nuova—for the Signorina Bianca Maria Marinelli. Would you like for me to summon your parents to hear it read, Bianca?"

"Yes, yes, please call them in," she said, her rising anger at Giacomo's words giving way to nervous excitement. Certainly she did not want to be alone with Fork-Beard for the news—whether good or bad.

Bianca sat waiting in silence, the large, folded parchment in her lap. Mercifully, Giacomo kept his silence, also. Then Albret ushered in her parents and bowed to dismiss himself. "No, please stay, Albret," Bianca said. He smiled, pleased to be a part of this momentous occasion.

Stefano rubbed his hands together and advised, "Remember, Bianca Maria, it remains a great honor just to have competed."

Bianca broke the seal. She read aloud: "From the committee for selecting an altarpiece for the Chiesa Nuova to the Signorina Bianca Maria Marinelli. This is to inform you that your painting, 'I Have Seen the Lord,' has been deemed by outside judges as the finest of the three entries and thus the one selected for the altarpiece. The dedication ceremonies will take place at the sanctuary this Sunday, August 1. We request that you prepare a short statement about your painting—explaining why you chose this subject and the message you hope to be instilled in the viewer. Only the members of the fellowship of Chiesa Nuova are invited, with the exception of your family and what friends you wish to invite. We, the undersigned committee, congratulate you on this very fine achievement."

"Praise be to God," said Stefano jubilantly. "I am so proud of your accomplishment, my daughter!"

"I sincerely hope this brings you happiness and not sorrow," said Françoise, tears forming.

"Good for you!" whispered Albret.

Giacomo cleared his throat. "I presume I am expected to be there?"

"Of course, Giacomo; I'm pleased you wish to be present in my support along with the rest of my family," Bianca said generously. "To all of you, thank you for your encouragement. I am truly humbled by this acclaim. God has simply used the talent He gave me to His glory."

eighteen

On this same Monday morning another important message was being delivered—to Marco Biliverti. His work had temporarily ceased at St. Peter's Basilica, as the architect had finished studying the present structure and was busily drafting his plans for the enlargement. Thus Marco was at home when a servant from the Biliverti Seignoiry arrived with a startling invitation from Jacopo: "Marco, please come with haste to the Biliverti castle so that together we may negotiate a settlement to this year-long struggle between brothers—without interference from bishops or any other authority. Come alone. I await your arrival."

So, Jacopo is, no doubt, aware that Bishop Ferrante has been asking questions in Terni. His vicious lies have been discovered, and thus he is ready to share our father's inheritance, thought Marco. *Well, I can be generous, but I must retain the castle for my mother and sister.*

He showed the message to Costanza and Anabella, who were excited at the prospect of soon going home, but at the same time showed concern for his safety.

Marco prepared for the trip, taking a two-day supply of food and water and a bedroll. The warmth of summer had set in, and sleeping under the stars would be pleasant. The family prayed together that evening, as Marco planned to slip out before dawn.

❧

The journey was agreeable, especially in the cool of the morning. Marco had always preferred the countryside to the busy city. By early afternoon, with the sun bearing down on his back, he stopped beside a river to rub down his horse. He found a delightful spot to take some nourishment, leaning against the trunk of a palm tree.

His thoughts drifted to Bianca. Last Sunday, Guido had whispered the decision of the judges to him, holding him to secrecy. She would have the news by now. The dedication of her painting was to take place the next Sunday. He must settle affairs with Jacopo and return in time to witness her moment of triumph.

Before continuing his journey, Marco shed his clothes and plunged into the river's refreshing waters for a brief swim. The heat of the afternoon dissipated as darkness fell. He had met few travelers during the day and was aware of the threat of bandits at night.

Therefore, he found a grassy spot away from the road to catch a few hours of sleep. Staring up at the stars, he pondered the miracle of creation and wondered what progress Galileo had made with his instrument to study the heavenly bodies. His university days seemed remote and unreal.

Then he contemplated his meeting with Jacopo. Perhaps his half brother would be reasonable. If only Marco could find the signed will his father had given him for safekeeping. Why had he left it in the secret wall panel of his room, vulnerable to theft, instead of bringing it with him to Rome? Then this dispute never could have taken place. He whispered a prayer and committed the next few days to God. Then he relived that bittersweet day when, among the Roman ruins, he had held the lovely Bianca in his arms. He gradually drifted into a deep slumber.

❧

Approaching his hometown late the next afternoon, Marco could hear the waterfall that was built by the ancient Romans, centuries before the birth of Christ, to divert the water of the Velino River. He recalled many an hour of his youth spent there with friends, but alas, there was no time for a detour. The quaint town boasted an amphitheater as well as other archaeological remains of centuries gone by. He rode past the old round church and saw the town's streets with new eyes, eyes that had been too long away from his roots.

His heart beat rapidly as the terraced vineyards of his seignoiry came into view. And then he beheld the castle of his childhood, crowning a rounded hill and silhouetted against the red sky of a summer sunset. He urged his horse into a gallop.

❧

The next morning found him disoriented, not recognizing at first his old room in the castle. Having slept more soundly than usual, he stretched and yawned. To his dismay, his left wrist and right ankle were cuffed and chained to the iron bed. Dismay gave way to gripping fear, bringing cold sweat to his brow. *What kind of welcome is this?* he questioned.

He recalled being met by a Spanish servant he didn't know last evening and being served an ample meal in the kitchen. The servant had informed him that he would meet with the Marchese Jacopo Biliverti on the morrow. Feeling fatigued after eating, he willingly let himself be led to his old bed-chamber. *But when were these shackles applied? Obviously, I have let myself into a trap,* he speculated.

Marco spent the morning in utter frustration and, finally, prayer. What did Jacopo have in mind? A gentle knock on the door interrupted his anxiety.

"Yes, I'm here," he called gruffly.

The door opened, revealing an elderly servant with a tray of food and drink. Indeed, this was the former chef of the castle. "Sandro!" Marco exclaimed, "how good. . ."

"Shhh. . . My orders are not to converse at all, but I must warn you. . . ," the old man whispered.

"Can you get these cursed chains off me?" pleaded Marco in a low voice.

"No, that would cost me my head, though it is of little value these days," he replied. Heavy footsteps in the hallway prompted the frightened Sandro to drop the tray on the bed and rush out, loudly slamming the door behind him.

All remained silent. Then the heavy footsteps retreated.

Marco found he had enough slack in the chains to eat—and to use the chamber pot under his bed. But what fate awaited him? Again fatigue overcame him, and he fell into a deep sleep.

As the shadows of dusk crept across his bed, Marco stirred and groaned. His muscles had stiffened in the grip of the chains. He opened his eyes, startled to see a thin and ominous figure hunched immobile in the shadows at his bedside.

"Well, my brother, I see you have soiled your bedclothes with your food tray. But you are the one who must sleep in it, not I." Apparently he had fallen asleep while eating. The figure laughed in a tone that lacked humor.

Marco sat up. "Jacopo, get these chains off me! Can we not sit civilly at a table and negotiate, brother to brother?"

"Eventually we can talk as brothers. I am having a dinner prepared in your honor tomorrow evening to celebrate our agreement. If this slight inconvenience of being chained to a comfortable bed can sway you to negotiate in fairness at this very moment, you will be free to go—or you can remain as an honored guest," said Jacopo, measuring his words.

"What is your proposal? Let us begin there," Marco said, hoping his calmness and openness might appease his foe.

"I demand the castle, one half the land, and one half the wealth. I believe that is what our father really would have wished. He became unreasonably upset when he learned of my lifestyle in Madrid. In his mind—in the fever of his illness—he exaggerated my indiscretions and irrationally withdrew my entire inheritance. Our father was a fair man. He never would have stooped to giving you everything in his sanity."

"In his sanity? Jacopo, our father was not at all ill, nor was he insane, when he had our scribe draw up his will." Marco was furious at the lies.

"I have here a codicil, penned by our same scribe, stating the facts I have just laid out. You must sign our father's name, as your script is nearer to his. They would accuse me of forgery, but never you. You realize that I am being exceedingly generous." Jacopo drew out the document, attached to the no-longer-missing will.

Instinctively, Marco tried to snatch the documents but was cruelly jerked back by the restraining chain.

"Will you sign now—or later under greater duress?" Jacopo asked as though he were offering the choice of bread or cake.

"Never, you evil thief!" Marco shouted, flinging himself back on the bed and pulling the covers over his head. The tray clattered to the floor.

"You will sign tomorrow evening at dinner. I have no more patience after that. Your fate will be your own choosing," Jacopo hissed between his teeth. Then he left, leaving Marco to unscramble this strange episode.

As his head cleared, Marco realized he had been drugged. The food must have contained a sleeping potion. Why? To keep him docile? He would refuse to eat from now on.

His reaction to Jacopo's proposal seemed extreme now that he was more alert. The division was not totally unfair, except he would fight to keep the castle for his family. But if forced to give that up, he could have a villa built on the far western side of the property. Why couldn't they sit down and negotiate like two gentlemen? Why was he being held prisoner? Why the lies about their father's wishes?

❧

Marco spent an agonizing night. No food had been brought for the evening meal, saving him from the temptation to eat. He lay in darkness. The soiled sheets reeked from the spilled tray. The iron cuffs could only be loosed with a key. Where were the loyal servants? Had all been dismissed and replaced by Spaniards, except for the frightened Sandro? He thrashed about and slept very little, if at all.

At midmorning, Sandro entered without knocking.

"I can't eat this, Sandro—take it away," Marco whispered. "For some reason Jacopo thinks I should sleep my life away, and has added something to my food. Did you know about this?"

"No, and I don't know about this meat," Sandro said, keeping a furtive eye on the door. "But I made the bread this morning and drew the water myself. At least take those. You will need to keep your strength. And there is something else. . . ."

"Yes?"

"Listen carefully. I risk danger even talking with you. You will be released for a gala dinner tonight with Jacopo. All the dishes will be pure, as I am to prepare them myself. But the wine. . .do not drink the wine. It will be tainted with a deadly poison. Another is to prepare it, and only I overheard the plot. Please, I beg you, do not reveal that it was I who told you of it."

"Not a word, I assure you, Sandro," whispered Marco. "I thank you for your risk." *So, he wants my life. There can be no good-faith negotiating now.*

≈

Back in Rome, Bianca had recovered completely from her exhaustion. She was in the midst of writing invitations to family friends, when Reginoldo burst into the sitting room.

"My sweet *sorellina*," he exclaimed, "how proud of you I am."

"Reginoldo, I am so happy you came," she said, embracing him with sincere affection.

"Everyone has seen your painting but me," he said. "Will you take me for a private showing?"

"I would love that, Reginoldo. Then I can practice my comments on you. You will let me know if it's all wrong, won't you?"

"Of course. But it will be perfect, I'm sure. You are the

authority, after all. And they are permitting a woman to stand up and say something in the church? I'm pleased, but that surprises me."

"It's not as if it were part of the service. I am just to explain a few points about how and why I did certain things in my work. Also, this is an unusual sort of church. I don't know much about it, but I know some of the members. Well, one, a certain Marco Biliverti. He tells me they accept everyone as equals. They feed the poor, visit hospitals, and do other good works with no respect to a person's status. They even study the Scriptures together. It was founded by someone named Neri, who is dead now. But he was a close friend of a high church official. So they are allowed a good deal of freedom."

"Interesting," commented Reginoldo. "And will your painting already be installed behind the altar?"

"No, I understand it will be displayed on an easel at the side of the chancel. The elaborate framing has not yet been completed."

Reginoldo turned to leave, then hesitated. Looking back at his sister, he said, "Bianca, dear *sorellina,* your eyes are sad amid this time of acclaim. Is it yet the betrothal?"

"Dear brother, yes, that overshadows any happiness that has come to me, but that is not all." In a scarcely audible voice, she added, "My heart belongs to another. I cannot speak of it. . . ."

Reginoldo waited a moment for her to continue. When she remained silent, he placed his hand lovingly on her shoulder. Then he left.

nineteen

For Marco, the hours dragged by. It was Friday. If he didn't make his escape tonight, he would never arrive in Rome for the dedication of Bianca's painting. At least she was safe among friends and family. She didn't really need him to be present. But he longed to be there, even with the pain of seeing her with another.

Finally, toward evening, four Spanish guards burst into his room. "You are to bathe and dress for dinner," said one. They unlocked the cuffs where they were attached to the bedposts, but left the chains attached to his wrist and ankle. Two men held the chains as Marco attended to his toilet. The other two stood with swords drawn. As he shaved himself, he was shocked at his own gaunt appearance in the mirror. From his armoire he selected an elegant maroon doublet and black trunk hosen.

The guards then led him downstairs to the dining hall, where a long table had been set with the family's finest dinnerware. Although the table could easily seat twelve, there were only two chairs, one at each end. A fully-lit candelabrum hung from a huge wooden beam over the center of the table. A guard attached the chain on his left wrist to the table leg. Much to Marco's surprise, his right leg was entirely released. The four guards then stood behind his chair.

Jacopo entered and placed a document within Marco's reach. He then seated himself at the other end of the table and placed a large ring with a single key on the table in front of him. Marco recognized his father's last will and testament. With a nod of his head, Jacopo dismissed the guards.

"Our father's signature, that you are to furnish, is your key to freedom. And this, dear Marco—well, it is a key, also," sneered Jacopo, "but it will only unlock your arm after the codicil is signed."

"Tell me, Jacopo, what were your intentions in following me around like a common spy in Rome?" Marco boldly asked.

Jacopo roared with laughter, "How clever of you, little brother, to spot me. Nevertheless, I learned much with which I can torture your mind if you do not do as I say. Concerning a certain Bianca Marinelli."

The chain pulled heavily on Marco's arm, and his whole body tensed in anger. He must somehow outsmart the beast. How dare he bring Bianca into this! At that moment, Sandro brought the first course—two exquisite plates of boiled quail's eggs in beef gelatin—and set them before the brothers. Weak from hunger, Marco devoured the delicacy in spite of his fears.

"It is a fine fare you serve, my brother, but a glass of wine would be a nice touch," said Marco, hoping to disconcert his foe.

"Hush, and sign the paper!" screamed Jacopo. "The wine will arrive in good time."

Keeping his eyes fastened on Jacopo, Marco reached for the document. He noted that the codicil had been folded and pinned to the will in such a way that only the area for the signature showed. Nevertheless, he dipped a quill in the ink container and signed, not his father's name, but the name Jacopo Biliverti.

Immediately one of the Spanish guards brought out two silver goblets. He set one at Marco's place, bowed slightly, then delivered the other to Jacopo.

"I propose a toast," said Marco, taking the initiative and lifting his goblet. "To our honorable deceased father. May his will forever be carried out."

Jacopo nodded. "To the intended will of our father."

As Jacopo lifted his goblet and drank, it was easy for Marco to simultaneously lift his and feign a sip. Jacopo's view was thus obscured by his own hand and goblet.

Jacopo relaxed, feeling complete success. But he could not resist one last boast before his brother would topple over. "And I have recently learned a fact about a certain Roberto Marinelli. I was hired to assassinate him." Then with an evil grimace, he pronounced these words slowly and deliberately: "He happened to be a brother of this little wench you've been squiring around."

Instead of toppling, Marco was filled with renewed energy by this most bitter of news. He stood abruptly and flung his goblet of wine toward Jacopo's face, at the same instant placing his entire weight on his end of the table. Plates and eating utensils slid toward him, down the length of the tilted table. And the coveted key!—it slipped right into his hand. Like lightening, he unlocked the cuff, grabbed the documents, and sped away—not toward the locked door, but down a little-used passageway that led to the storage cellars.

There sat the ladder he had used dozens of times as a child to crawl out the high window. On this hot summer night, it was open. The guards—rapiers drawn—were behind him as he reached the window. He kicked the ladder in their faces and slid down the familiar tree.

Now if only his horse would be in the corral where he had left him with a stable hand he once had trusted. As he rushed toward the enclosure, he could see the outline of a man standing beside a horse. Friend or foe? He would take his chances.

"Aye, Marco, I expected you, but not so soon. Your horse is bridled, but I was just going for the saddle. . . ." The familiar voice was quick and husky.

"No time, my good man. Thank you for the risk you've taken," said Marco between quick breaths as he tore away on the horse.

Rather than follow the road through Terni, he disappeared into the dense pine forest. Marco knew every inch of this countryside. There was a riding path that entered the trees a short distance ahead, but for now he must dismount and lead his horse through the underbrush and overhanging branches. Horsemen in pursuit would have difficulty making it through here.

Once on the riding path, he tore away at high speed.

❦

Entering the narthex of Chiesa Nuova, Bianca felt odd on the arm of Giacomo Villani. Little had she realized that for the first time they would be seen as a couple by many of their friends and acquaintances. The praise for her achievement was thus overshadowed by felicitations on their betrothal. Giacomo, who had remained sullen up to this point, began to nod, smile, and thank the well-wishers for their kind words. It was apparent he felt no need at the moment to be ashamed of this one so highly honored.

Bianca scanned the crowd for Marco without success. Finally, as they were filing into the nave, Anabella grabbed her hand. "We love your painting," she whispered.

Bianca gave her hand a squeeze of acknowledgment and stopped for a quick introduction of her betrothed. Costanza quickly sized up the situation and let Bianca read the disappointment in her face. This was the young woman meant only for her son. "My son is away in Terni," she said to answer Bianca's unspoken question. "He has, however, seen and admired your magnificent painting."

"It is truly magnificent, isn't it?" said Giacomo as though he had painted it himself. *Although he has never, until now, bothered to come view it,* thought Bianca bitterly.

"Please accompany us on the front pews," offered Bianca. Stefano also had invited the Gentileschis as well as Lavinia Zapponi and her husband to sit with them. As they settled into their places, Artemisia inquired about Bianca's health. Being assured that all was well, she whispered, "You surely didn't paint that, did you?" The girls exchanged smirks over their private joke. Anabella managed to glance at the row behind her and exchange warm smiles with Albret.

Bianca entered into the liturgy with enthusiasm. Every word had personal meaning to her now. Since that morning in the studio when she had sought the Lord's guidance in finishing the painting, He had seemed so very real. Every day she prayed to Him sincerely from the heart. She was filled with assurance that whatever the future held, God would be with her. Being married to Giacomo was the worst thing she could imagine, but if it was God's will, she could surely bear it. At least she had been granted a taste of true love. She was certain Marco loved her as strongly as she loved him.

So much had changed in the year since she had sat in her own church for the dedication of the St. Matthew paintings by Caravaggio. She recalled how mesmerized she had been by his sheer talent. Now, she, too, had painted to God's glory. In disbelief she gazed at her own painting. Beyond the joke with Artemisia, she truly marveled that her hand could possibly have produced it.

The service drew all too quickly to a close. The time had come for Bianca's "words." Françoise patted her knee. Reginoldo and Stefano appeared prouder than ever. The lay priest had a few words of his own about how pleased they were with their new altarpiece. He thanked the committee and the judges for their diligence and discrimination in their choice. "I give you now our young artist, Bianca Maria Marinelli," he said with enthusiasm.

Alas, Bianca's damp palms had smudged the words of her speech beyond recognition. She stuck the little wad of paper in her sleeve and stood before her audience. With a voice steady and clear, she began, "To the parishioners of Chiesa Nuova, my family and friends, I humbly thank you for your kind words of praise. But it is to the glory of our Lord Jesus Christ that I have. . ."

Suddenly a loud clatter from the narthex broke off her

sentence. Then six armed men burst into the nave and strode up the aisles. One shouted, "Halt this procedure in the name of all that is holy!" Bianca stood stunned, immobile. Two policemen grabbed her arms and escorted her out of the church. Another, in a loud voice, intoned, "Remain in your places. Anyone who moves will be arrested." The four then proceeded to remove the canvas from its easel. Stefano and Françoise, both struck dumb with anguish, sat with their eyes riveted to the doorway through which their daughter had passed—as though witnessing the end of the world.

When the painting was carried out, Reginoldo leapt to his feet. Motioning the others to remain seated, he dashed after the officers. Outside he saw Bianca sitting tightly between the two officers in a cart for common criminals. As they pulled away, he noticed the others prying the canvas from its frame. He approached them with open palms to show he held no weapon. "*Signors,* please, there is a mistake. The lady is Bianca Marinelli, and I am her brother. What crime could she possibly be accused of?"

"Ah, you would go to the Tor di Nona prison? You also?" sneered one.

"You see I am not armed. As her family, we have the right to know the accusation." Then he shouted, "You have just burst into a holy church during service. Surely you know that if the high church officials learn of how you have profaned God's house. . ."

At these words the four men crossed themselves. One then quickly rolled up the canvas, jumped on his steed, and followed the cart.

"All right, then tell the officials that the arrest happened out here," said one, not wanting his eternity endangered.

"Yes? Go on."

"It seems this here canvas was stolen, right from the studio of Michele Merisi da Caravaggio just after he ran from justice. It was sitting on his easel, it was. The girl finished it and claimed it as her own. The Cardinal del Monte of the Palazzo Madama is convinced of it. He's a patron of the artist, you know, and is protecting his personal goods."

"And how, pray tell, could a mere young lady. . .?" protested Reginoldo.

"Ah ha! No, it was a certain nobleman, you understand, who purloined it in the dead of night," explained another policeman.

"And his name would be?"

"Get along with ye now. That's all we know. She'll have her day in court before the tribunal. And don't forget, the arrest took place right here, where we're standing." The remaining police rode off after the others.

Reginoldo rushed back to the alarmed congregation. Quieting the group, he relayed what little information he had learned. "It is total falsehood, I can assure you," he added. "We must quickly get to the bottom of this."

Lavinia then stood and, though trembling with shock, stated loudly and clearly, "Please, don't any of you believe there is truth to this charge. I am Bianca's tutor. I have watched her from sketch to completion. There is not a speck of truth to this horrendous accusation."

The lay priest then came forward. "There were such rumors before today. None of us here at the fellowship took them seriously. The committee and judges are all convinced this is an untruth. We are as shocked as her family and friends," he said. "Now, if you think you can be of help in clearing this honorable, young lady, please stay. The rest of you are free to go in peace. The officers have left."

Françoise wept uncontrollably. "I knew this would come to a bad end," she moaned.

Costanza tugged the sleeve of Stefano. "The nobleman that he mentioned," she whispered, "just might refer to my son Marco. He would not have done such a deed, but perhaps. . ."

"Perhaps. Yes, there might be some sort of connection,

somehow," said Stefano, trying desperately to sort out everything. "Where is Marco, anyway?"

"His brother invited him to Terni. You know about that conflict, I presume," she said, wanting to help and, at the same time, not wanting to risk Marco's safety. "He had planned to be back in time for the dedication."

"Do you realize that the police will be searching for him, also?"

A look of alarm crossed her face. "Marco was often in Caravaggio's studio," she confided.

"Reginoldo, we must form a search party to find Marco," Stefano told his son, who had been intensely listening to everyone's opinions.

"Marco who?"

"Never mind. I'll explain later. Just get a group of loyal men together—with weapons—and have them meet at our villa in an hour," ordered Stefano.

When the Marinelli couple arrived at home, Françoise gave in to hysterics. "Now, now, Françoise, my sweet wife, we must be strong for Bianca Maria's sake," said Stefano in an effort to comfort. "Sylvia, do something."

As Sylvia put her arms around her, Stefano was off to dress more suitably for riding—and to pick up his rapier. He would lead the search party toward Terni and intercept Marco.

twenty

The Tor di Nona, etched against the graying sky of evening, stood like a monster ready to devour the cart as it approached. Bianca had sat still as death between her two captors, who jested and guffawed on a variety of topics, none of which pertained to her. They neither harassed nor treated her cruelly, but fear tore at her heart.

Inside, she was led up a circular, stone staircase, dank and foreboding. The men shoved her into a nine-foot-square room as if they were depositing a sack of grain for another to pick up. The door clanked behind her, and she heard that most frightful of sounds—the drop of a bar that locked her within. Their voices faded, and she heard their boots descend the stairs.

Bianca Maria Marinelli—the acclaimed artist—stood alone in the middle of the cell. Old straw, reeking with horrible odors, covered the floor. Eerie light from the high, barred window let her long shadow stretch out in front of her. A rustle in the straw alerted her to the small inhabitants that shared this space. Soon total darkness would engulf the room. Glancing to one side, she saw a pallet. She approached and knelt on it, tucking her skirts around her. How could she ever lie where criminals had lain? Her heart beat wildly, as though it would burst.

Then from the core of her being, she raised a prayer directly to God without the filter of words. Soon peace like a mantle fell across her shoulders. No longer was she alone.

She tried to recall what had happened. Much remained blacked out in her mind. But her arrest somehow must concern the painting. As the men were pushing her onto the cart, she had glanced over her shoulder, half-expecting the entire congregation to come rushing to her rescue. Instead, she

154

remembered seeing her masterpiece being dragged out the portals.

One of the officers had said something—not to her specifically—about how a woman could never hope to pass off as her own a great man's work. Later, on the way to the prison, there was a snatch of a phrase. . .something along the lines of "they'll find the rest of Caravaggio's work." At the time, she thought it had nothing to do with her, but now she put the two together. *Do they think I stole the painting from Caravaggio?*

№

Marco had ridden swiftly through the pine forest all night long, after coming upon the path he knew so well. It would soon join the main road, affording him less protection. The sun would be uncomfortably hot in a couple of hours. Why not take a respite while still sheltered by the forest? He dismounted and led his horse away from the path.

After tying his steed, he fell exhausted to the ground. But he had just enough energy remaining to satisfy his curiosity about the codicil he had signed his brother's name to—unread. He pulled it from his doublet and removed the pin. Following the preliminaries, he read, "Therefore, the attached last will and testament is now null and void, being thus replaced with that of my original desire: that the castle, all lands, and all wealth be bestowed unequivocally upon my older son, Jacopo Biliverti." *So Jacopo had no intention of dividing with me at all. In fact, he intended to take my life.* Hunger and thirst gnawed at his insides until he fell asleep.

Suddenly he awoke to the thundering of horses' hooves. He sat up just in time to see a posse of perhaps six to eight men ride down the path in single file. They had followed his bypass precisely. Now they posed an even greater danger for they might return to face him at any juncture. He sat too far away to tell if Jacopo was in the group. At any rate, he must exercise extreme caution.

With no money and no weapon, Marco felt vulnerable to

all sorts of misfortunes as he rode from the forest path to the main road. Here, there was no place to hide. At every turn, he would expect to encounter the thundering posse.

❧

Finally, the cover of night eased his fears. At least he would be harder to recognize, and if he could remain alert, he would hear them first and exit the road. *If I can remain alert. Dear Lord, please see me safely to Rome.*

Then he heard them—the thundering hooves. Not thinking clearly, he abruptly jerked the reins across his horse's neck. The steed reared and whinnied loudly. Instead of exiting the road, he whirled about and galloped off in the opposite direction. With no saddle to cradle Marco's weakened body, he fell with a thud in front of the oncoming horsemen.

❧

One by one, friends and parishioners arrived at the Marinelli household. "Are they all here, Reginoldo?" Stefano asked his son, eager to be off.

"All but Giacomo."

"But he came home with us. Where. . .?"

Heavy boots descending the staircase answered Stefano's question before it was uttered. Giacomo carried his bag of belongings and approached Stefano with deliberate steps.

"What is it, man? Out with it. We must. . ."

"Signor Marinelli, I mean no disrespect. No disrespect to you at all. I understand that unfortunate events happen," Giacomo stammered, avoiding eye contact.

"Yes, go on," Stefano said, hardly masking his irritation with this tardiness.

"I ask that I be relieved from this betrothal to your daughter. You see. . ."

"I see perfectly, coward!" shouted Stefano, his irritation turning to rage. "Get out of my house! You have defiled my dead son's room with your very presence. How could I have been so blind as not to see what a lowly beast I was unknowingly foisting on my precious Bianca Maria! Out!"

Giacomo made a quick exit as all the men stared in disbelief at this most fainthearted soul. Merely uttering his daughter's name brought a surge of emotion to the father's tender heart. But he must be brave and lead. He dared not let his mind imagine the horror she must be enduring. "Let us be off!" he shouted with authority.

❧

Pain shot through Marco's left shoulder as he lay helpless to defend himself. The thundering posse roared toward him at full speed. Instinctively he raised his right arm. Whatever evil intent they had for him, his immediate wish was not to be trampled. Then he passed out.

❧

Marco opened his eyes to see two strangers leaning over him. He lay on his back looking up at tops of palm trees. Was it the twilight of evening or early morning? Where was he? No doubt Jacopo's guards had brought him here. He made an effort to sit up.

"No, rest, Marco," said one of the strangers. "You have been unconscious. Your shoulder is injured, but we think it is not broken."

"Who are you?"

"We are new at the fellowship and have been so thankful for their help that we volunteered to search for you."

At that moment, Stefano knelt beside him and pressed a cup of water to his lips. "You fell from your horse just as we approached," he said. "You seemed to fear us and attempted to turn back."

"Indeed, I was in need of rescue, but I don't understand why you would have come for me."

"There is much to tell, Marco, but it can wait until after you've eaten some breakfast."

One mystery solved, thought Marco. *It's morning, not evening.*

èa

Being young and strong, Marco quickly revived after food, water, and a little rest. Fortunately, his horse wandered back into camp just as the men saddled up. Reginoldo loaned him his saddle, as Marco's upper arm was bound tight against his body by strips of cloth, making bareback riding especially difficult. So heavy was Stefano's heart that he asked Reginoldo to relate for Marco the terrifying event at the church—concluding with Bianca's arrest. It deeply pained Marco that the lovely Bianca should be subjected to such terror, especially at her moment of triumph. His recent imprisonment in his own castle was *nothing* compared to what she must endure in the state prison. *Oh, Bianca, my love, if only I could protect you.*

As they rode along, Reginoldo explained their plan to Marco. When they approached Rome, they would follow different routes, traveling in pairs for safety. He had even brought along a floppy hat and false mustache for Marco. "We suspect you are the nobleman they will be looking for," Reginoldo said. "It is time for you to don these."

Marco pressed the black mustache to his upper lip.

"By the way, another bit of news. Giacomo has asked my father to be released from his betrothal to Bianca."

"And he agreed?" Fetters fell from Marco's heart, which leapt with joy. *I must not let her slip away again. I'll not rest until I have this most cruel misunderstanding solved.*

"He ordered him out of our house! Yes, I would say there is no longer a betrothal," said Reginoldo, happy to share the news with willing ears.

èa

Reginoldo, being less known in the city than any of the others, was chosen to accompany Marco to the Marinelli villa. Once arrived, the two men stabled their horses and slipped in the side entrance. A few minutes later, Stefano came in by way of the front gate. Françoise bustled about and brought the three men food and drink. Calmer now, she sat at their table in anticipation of sharing her small bit of the puzzle at the right moment.

"We must first consider what reasons one may have for making such an outlandish charge against. . .against Bianca Maria." Stefano buried his face in his hands, obviously overcome with emotion.

"Perhaps it was the jealousy of the other two artists," offered Reginoldo. "They presented work that was certainly worthy of consideration. Does anyone know anything about them?"

"Nothing, other than that they are both young and unknown, like Bianca," said Marco. "I know a member of the committee who chose them for the competition. I could approach him. He is usually at the church."

"No, you must stay here, in hiding," said Stefano, seemingly recovered now from his emotional lapse.

"But is that safe? Officers may come here, looking for who knows what," said Reginoldo.

"Two have already been here. This morning," interjected Françoise, recognizing the right moment. "They said they were looking for the rest of Caravaggio's stolen canvases. They tore through Bianca's room. I pointed out that the painting in question bore a similarity to the *cassone,* which obviously never belonged to any Caravaggio."

"How brave of you, Françoise!" exclaimed Stefano. "You must have been terrified with two officers rummaging through this house."

"The time for tears has past," said Françoise resolutely. "They did study the *cassone,* but thought it far inferior to the painting, and thus it could not have been accomplished by the same. . ."

"I have proof!" Marco said suddenly with conviction. "Bianca gave me the sketch she made for 'I Have Seen the Lord.' It hangs above my bed, signed and dated."

Stefano's eyebrows shot up.

"I'll ride to your house to fetch it," offered Reginoldo. "Your mother and sister will be happy to know of your welfare."

"Also, I have been in contact with a certain Bishop Ferrante who has been helpful to me in another legal matter," said Marco, energized by his recall of the sketch. "If he could present the drawing to the papal tribunal, it would lend credence to our cause."

Discussion then gave way to action.

Reginoldo rode off quickly on his mission to the Biliverti residence.

Marco hastily wrote a message for Bishop Ferrante and sent it by Albret.

And Stefano wondered why Bianca Maria's sketch would be hanging above Marco's bed.

⁂

Bishop Ferrante, busy with many matters, had sadly neglected Marco's case. However, he was intrigued by the turn of events that now involved the possible theft of a Caravaggio painting. A lifetime friend of Cardinal del Monte, the artist's patron, he made a call at the Palazzo Madama, where he was quickly granted private audience.

"What made you think this young lady, Bianca Marinelli, would have purloined a canvas from Caravaggio's studio?" Ferrante asked as they shared refreshment.

"A certain man by the name of Jacopo Biliverti called on me with a letter of introduction by our friend, Bishop Mariano. . . ."

"Your friend, not mine. We are on opposite sides of nearly every issue," Ferrante interrupted. "In fact, strange as it may seem, Mariano represents this Jacopo in a property dispute. And I represent Marco, his half brother."

"How strange, also, that they both have an interest in the theft of this painting. Jacopo told me he had seen Marco climb through the window of the studio one night and leave with several rolls of what appeared to be canvases. Claims he followed his brother Marco because of threats Marco had made on his life. How can one determine the truth?"

"I'm not sure why this involves them both. But according to a message I have just received from Marco, he has in his possession the sketch, signed and dated, of the painting in question, made by the young lady."

"That would almost certainly prove it was her creation and not Caravaggio's. Is he able to bring it here for scrutiny?"

❦

When summoned to the Palazzo Madama by the Cardinal del Monte, Marco insisted on risking his own arrest to deliver the sketch. The cardinal immediately recognized the drawing as being the precursor to the painting, having privately viewed it at the Chiesa Nuova. Together with Bishop Ferrante's report on the wicked character of Jacopo, he was convinced that the story was false and immediately withdrew his charges against Bianca—for indeed it was the cardinal who had made them.

❦

A joyful group it was, descending the road that led away from the Tor di Nona. Albret drove the carriage. Beside him sat Reginoldo, and behind them, the freed Bianca, pressed between her adoring father and the young man who loved her with all his heart.

"Yes, it was a horrible experience," she said in answer to their many questions. "But the Lord was with me. And I am so blessed to have all of you to fight for me."

"We suffered every horrible moment with you," said Marco, his heart bursting with thankfulness for her release.

"But not everyone has such a wonderful family and friends," said Bianca, her voice taking on a tone of sadness. "A few hours before my release, they brought a young widow to share my cell. She had stolen some fruit and bread for her hungry children. I've never been that close to the miseries of others— not of that sort. I know, Marco, how you helped the little orphan girl and so many others. Do you suppose we could help that widow somehow?"

"I was blind to such misery myself until the fellowship taught me how God wants us as Christians to let His love flow through us to others," said Marco. "Yes, they often pay the fine to release such unfortunates from the prison. I'll see what we can do."

"Young men from that fellowship who had never met Marco risked their lives to warn him," said Stefano. "I do believe they have found what serving God is all about."

Reginoldo and Albret heartily agreed.

twenty-one

Safe at home at last, Bianca relaxed in the sitting room with her parents, who hovered over her with loving concern, anticipating her every need.

"I'm really fine. I'm not an invalid," she finally said. "Look what I found in my sleeve—the little speech I was to make at the dedication. Let's see if I can make out the words."

"Do read it to us," said Stefano, even more proud of his daughter at this moment than when she had stood before the congregation.

Bianca read what she could and remembered the rest: "To the parishioners of Chiesa Nuova, my family and friends, I humbly thank you for your kind words of praise. But it is to the glory of our Lord Jesus Christ that I have been able to create this altarpiece. You see Mary Magdalene bathed in the light and love of Jesus after He rose from the dead on Easter morn. The expression of awe and reverence on her face comes from the realization that her Lord loved her so much that He appeared before her and called her name, 'Mary.' Thus each of us, as we look to Christ, can be assured that He indeed does love and call us personally by name. That is what I want you to think about as you look upon this painting."

They both clapped in approval.

"Bianca, I have something to say," said Françoise, beaming with as much pride as her husband. "When they took you away, I thought, in my grief, that I had been right to try to shield you from just this sort of thing. But I have been wrong. I admire your courage. God certainly did bless you with a wonderful gift, and you have truly used it to His glory. God Himself revealed that to me as I prayed almost constantly for your safety."

"Thank you, Mother. Those are precious words to me."

"I even dug up some of my old compositions and played them while you were gone. I really no longer have any desire to publish them. But you have given me courage to compose again."

"Maybe I am beginning to understand some things about women," said Stefano, nervously crossing and uncrossing his legs.

"And, pray tell, how is that?" said Françoise.

"Well, they certainly are as brave as men. And in this family, at least, ever so talented. And I have a confession to make." He hesitated and glanced at both of them for approval to go on— which they willingly gave.

"Like you two, I had a notion of my future as a young man. Although I have done very well in banking, what I always dreamed of. . ."

"Yes, go on," his wife and daughter said in unison.

"Well, I always dreamed of having a home in the country. You know, cows, growing things, vineyards. . .I guess that's hard to understand," he said shyly.

"Not at all, Stefano, since much of your boyhood was spent on a farm in *la belle France,*" said Françoise, putting her arms around his shoulders and kissing him lovingly on the lips.

For Bianca, this was the kind of moment she had always wished for—her parents sharing openly with each other and with her. "Well, it's time to leave you two. I'll ask Sylvia to heat my bath," she said, heading toward the stairs.

"Good night, Bianca," said Françoise. "We love you so."

"We do," added Stefano. "And, by the way, I invited Marco and his mother and sister for dinner tomorrow night. I thought we all needed a celebration."

Bianca, tired as she was from her awful ordeal, felt a completeness to her joy. Fork-beard was gone from her life forever. And tomorrow night Marco would be here.

❧

Unlike another dinner occasion, Bianca involved herself completely in the planning and preparation of this one. But a certain nervousness had set in. Before, there had always been a forbidden wall between herself and Marco. She'd had a sense of freedom in speaking her mind and heart because, after all, they could never belong to each other. A wrong word here or there couldn't really matter.

Now, without that wall, they might see each other differently. Françoise teased her daughter about paying so much attention to detail in the preparations, but at the same time, the two women had never worked together in so much happiness. Finally, when the Bilivertis arrived and Bianca was in the presence of Marco, a calmness came over her spirit. All was well.

At the table, the two families laughed and shared stories from the past. Costanza related how Marco as a young boy used to climb out a high window from the cellars and escape down a tree during siesta time.

"Mother, how did you know? I thought that was my private antic!"

"Mothers know," she said, rolling her eyes knowingly at Françoise.

Then Reginoldo observed, "Looks as if I won't need to kick anyone's shins tonight."

"But I'll have to kick yours!" Bianca laughed at their private sibling joke over Fork-Beard's family.

After enjoying Bianca's raspberry dessert, artistically presented, the men retired to the sitting room. Bianca invited Costanza and Anabella to her room to show them the panel on her *cassone,* taken from Anabella's pose at the Piazza del Popolo. She even dared open the chest and reveal its contents in response to Anabella's curiosity. The child was delighted with the beautiful needlework, being gifted in that domestic art herself.

It had been opened only once in the three years since Roland died. That had been to slip in a small *cloisonné* case that held a precious bunch of pressed orchids.

❧

When the ladies returned, Marco was waiting at the bottom of the stairs. In her pale yellow dress embroidered in blue flowers, her dark curls tied back and cascading over her shoulders, eyes shining, Bianca appeared the most radiant and beautiful he could remember. He suggested they walk out into the courtyard. There, the full moon poured out its defused light; the roses in their Grecian urns spread their fragrance; and the distant notes of a harpsichord drifted through the opened doorway.

"Who is playing that sweet music?" asked Marco.

"My mother. I believe she composed it herself, as it is a piece I've never heard."

Bianca then shared her mother's story. Marco told her of his adventure with Jacopo at the castle. Bianca thanked him for all he had done on her behalf to obtain her release. She said she had been notified that her painting had been recovered and would soon be installed. Marco told how he had sought out the lay pastors at the fellowship; if she would like, they could accompany them to the prison to gain the release of the widow Bianca had met there. There seemed to be no end to what they yearned to share and learn from each other. The words tumbled out like water endlessly flowing from a Roman fountain.

Then suddenly, silence fell—except for Françoise's far-off playing. They stood, watching the silver-edged clouds slide across the moon. Then Marco turned to Bianca and slipped his hands around her waist. He pulled her close. Melting into his arms, she returned his embrace.

"We've been too long apart," he whispered.

"I know," she said, turning her face up to his.

"I love you," he breathed and blended his lips with hers.

The earth stopped in midrotation. Stars shone brighter. And Bianca was sure she heard angels singing to her mother's playing. *This is the kind of love Sylvia said was possible,* she thought. *Never did I think I would know it for myself.*

They stood wrapped together, consumed by the bliss of the moment.

"I love you, Bianca. I want you to be my wife. When you are ready."

Feeling faint, Bianca sat on the stone bench. Marco joined her and took her hand. "I know how much your painting means to you, Bianca—I would never take that away from you. And you've said you didn't want to marry, but I must return to my home soon—the castle and land are mine now, and I need to take mother and 'Bella there—there is so much business to take care of—I must record my father's will, though now there is no longer a contest—you could study another year with Lavinia and I will come as often as. . ."

Bianca lay her finger on his lips. "Hush, Marco. You are babbling. I do love you, and I *didn't* want to marry. But what sad pictures I would paint, separated from you for a whole year!"

"Then does that mean you will marry me?"

"We will have to ask Papa, you know."

"I already have his permission!" exclaimed Marco triumphantly. "What do you think we men were discussing in the sitting room—bullfights and politics?"

Bianca chuckled. "Then I have no choice. I promised God I would not go against my parents wishes. Yes, Marco—yes, I will marry you."

Marco brushed a ringlet from her cheek and met her warm, moist lips with his. Then he lightly kissed her forehead, and she lay her head on his shoulder.

Suddenly she recalled his injury from falling off his horse. "Oh, I am sorry; I forgot. Does your shoulder still give you pain?" she asked, raising her head.

"Not this one, it's the other. And if it did, I would endure it for the joy of having your head against it."

"You are, indeed, romantic, Marco," she said. She smiled, snuggling her head back onto his good shoulder. Then more seriously, she added, "What did you mean awhile ago when you said there was no more contest over your castle?"

Marco took both her hands in his. "Just today, a servant from the seignoiry brought me a letter that had arrived in Terni months ago. While here, he told me of happenings that followed my recent departure. Jacopo became deranged after being drenched with the poisoned wine that I 'returned' to him. He tore his clothes, thinking the poison would kill him, even though it never touched his lips. I believe his rage sprang from having his plan foiled—or maybe even from guilt. Rather than join the posse he sent after me, he rode off in another direction, alone, screaming obscenities. Not far from the castle, he was set upon by bandits and murdered for the bag of coins he carried."

"He was your brother. I'm sorry."

"Half brother. I'm sorry, too. I was willing to share with him. But I can understand why our father cut off his inheritance. Verily, he was an evil man." Marco decided to wait for a more opportune time to tell Bianca of Jacopo's worst crime—*murdering her brother, Roberto, for hire.*

"Anyhow, there is much work to oversee at the seignoiry. As the vineyards had not been properly tended, the harvest was scanty this year. I sent word back by the servant that I would return within a week. All the former servants and workers who are still there are to remain. I'm sure Jacopo's Spanish guards have already left. If you are willing, we could be married within a few weeks."

"That sounds all too wonderful."

"We'll find a place at the castle where you can set up your studio. I want you to use your talent."

"Thank you, Marco. I do want to continue painting, but I

will have many more concerns now. With you, I can live happily on both sides of the easel." Her heart's desire, she discovered, was no longer so narrowly focused.

Then, thinking of what Marco had given up, she asked, "Have you ever considered returning to the university?"

"Well, that brings up a subject I had planned for later. We do have the rest of our lives, you know. Everything doesn't have to be said tonight, dearest Bianca."

"But I want to know everything about you, all at once. Tell me about the university."

"The letter our servant brought was from the professor I so admired, Galileo. He has invited a small group of select students to come to Padua for a couple of months this winter. He wants us to work with him on some scientific experiments. Once I get the seigniory running smoothly, we could rent a small place near the university. There is an art colony there, and I'm sure you could find a good tutor—if you still need one."

"Life will always be exciting with you, Marco, whatever we do and wherever we live."

Marco took his beloved in his arms once more. "I think I've loved you since that moment our eyes met on the steps of the Santa Suzanna. You seemed to carry the whole city of Rome in the palm of your hand."

"I think I loved you then, too. But I was looking past you to grandeur."

"It's getting late. Shall we go in and tell our families that this celebration is never to end? They had better all like each other, for they will soon be relatives!"

"Our families are a good blend, don't you think, Marco?"

"I do."

author's notes

Caravaggio died in 1610 in Port Ercole, a Spanish province, three days before a document of clemency arrived from Rome.

Caravaggio's three paintings of St. Matthew still hang in the Contarelli Chapel in the Church of San Luigi dei Francesi in Rome.

Caravaggio's "St. John the Baptist in the Wilderness" is featured in the Masters Collection of the Nelson-Atkins Museum of Art in Kansas City, Missouri.

A Letter To Our Readers

Dear Reader:

In order that we might better contribute to your reading enjoyment, we would appreciate your taking a few minutes to respond to the following questions. We welcome your comments and read each form and letter we receive. When completed, please return to the following:

Rebecca Germany, Fiction Editor
Heartsong Presents
PO Box 719
Uhrichsville, Ohio 44683

1. Did you enjoy reading *Both Sides of the Easel* by Barbara Youree?
   ❑ Very much! I would like to see more books by this author!
   ❑ Moderately. I would have enjoyed it more if

_____

_____

2. Are you a member of **Heartsong Presents**? Yes ❑ No ❑
   If no, where did you purchase this book?_____

_____

3. How would you rate, on a scale from 1 (poor) to 5 (superior), the cover design?_____

4. On a scale from 1 (poor) to 10 (superior), please rate the following elements.

   _____ Heroine   _____ Plot

   _____ Hero   _____ Inspirational theme

   _____ Setting   _____ Secondary characters

5. These characters were special because_____

_____

_____

6. How has this book inspired your life?_____

_____

_____

7. What settings would you like to see covered in future **Heartsong Presents** books?_____

_____

_____

8. What are some inspirational themes you would like to see treated in future books?_____

_____

_____

9. Would you be interested in reading other **Heartsong Presents** titles?　　　Yes ❏　　　　　No ❏

10. Please check your age range:
　　❏ Under 18　　❏ 18-24　　❏ 25-34
　　❏ 35-45　　　❏ 46-55　　❏ Over 55

11. How many hours per week do you read?_____

Name _____

Occupation _____

Address _____

City _____ State _____ Zip _____

"Let your light so shine before men,
that they may see your good works,
and glorify your Father which is in heaven."
MATTHEW 5:16

Introducing a brand new historical novella collection
with four female lighthouse
keepers, at four different points
of the compass in the United
States. Each woman will need to
learn to trust in God and the
guidance of His Light as they
seek to do their appointed tasks.
Salting their characters' lives with
romance, the authors bring each
of these tales to an expected yet
miraculous ending.

When Love Awaits by Lynn A. Coleman
A Beacon in the Storm by Andrea Boeshaar
Whispers Across the Blue by DiAnn Mills
A Time to Love by Sally Laity

paperback, 352 pages, 5 ³⁄₁₆" x 8"

❤ • ❤ • ❤ • ❤ • ❤ • ❤ • **❤** • ❤ • ❤ • ❤ • ❤ • ❤ • ❤

❤ • ❤ • ❤ • ❤ • ❤ • ❤ • **❤** • ❤ • ❤ • ❤ • ❤ • ❤ • ❤

·······Presents·······

Great Inspirational Romance at a Great Price!

Heartsong Presents books are inspirational romances in contemporary and historical settings, designed to give you an enjoyable, spirit-lifting reading experience. You can choose wonderfully written titles from some of today's best authors like Peggy Darty, Sally Laity, Tracie Peterson, Colleen L. Reece, Lauraine Snelling, and many others.

When ordering quantities less than twelve, above titles are $2.95 each.
Not all titles may be available at time of order.

Hearts♥ng Presents
Love Stories Are Rated G!

That's for godly, gratifying, and of course, great! If you love a thrilling love story, but don't appreciate the sordidness of some popular paperback romances, **Heartsong Presents** is for you. In fact, **Heartsong Presents** is the *only inspirational romance book club* featuring love stories where Christian faith is the primary ingredient in a marriage relationship.

Sign up today to receive your first set of four, never before published Christian romances. Send no money now; you will receive a bill with the first shipment. You may cancel at any time without obligation, and if you aren't completely satisfied with any selection, you may return the books for an immediate refund!

Imagine. . .four new romances every four weeks—two historical, two contemporary—with men and women like you who long to meet the one God has chosen as the love of their lives. . . all for the low price of $9.97 postpaid.

To join, simply complete the coupon below and mail to the address provided. **Heartsong Presents** romances are rated G for another reason: They'll arrive *Godspeed!*